Praise for JEDIDIAH AYRES & PECKERWOOD:

"*Peckerwood* is intensely original and harrowing country noir. Ayres delivers sharp-edged prose that lands like a knife under the ribs."
– Dennis Tafoya, author of *Dope Thief* and *The Poor Boy's Game*

"A masterpiece of dirty, down-low rural noir. Read it and sink a little further into the muck."
– Scott Phillips, author of *The Ice Harvest* and *Rake*

"Some people find comfort in religion, booze, sex, drugs. I don't judge. But I find comfort in Jedidiah Ayres."
– Benjamin Whitmer, author of *Pike* and co-author of *Satan is Real: The Ballad of the Louvin Brothers*

"Jedidiah Ayres combines a crooked world view and a dark turn of mind with a genuine, increasingly rare pulse of humanity to create stories that stand apart."
– Sean Doolittle, author of *The Cleanup* and *Lake Country*

"One of the most innovative crime fiction writers currently on the scene."
– *LitReactor*

A Broken River Books original

Broken River Books
103 Beal Street
Norman, OK 73069

Interior design by J David Osborne

Excerpts from *Peckerwood* first appeared in *Thuglit*, *Crime Factory*, and *Noir at the Bar Vol. 2*.

ISBN: 978-1-940885-01-8

Printed in the USA.

PECKERWOOD
JEDIDIAH AYRES

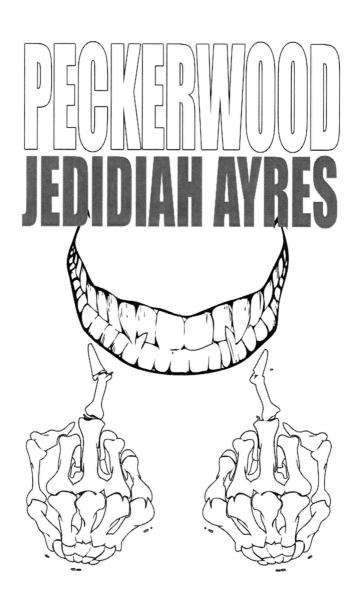

BROKEN RIVER BOOKS
NORMAN, OK

For Cort McMeel

PART I

If Terry Hickerson had had a working doorbell in the front of his place it wouldn't have rung anyway. It was one of those nagging bits of faulty or expired equipment he always seemed to be surrounded by. He was constantly leveraging the value of his precious time and energy against the odds that he'd ever need a functional whatsit again, appreciating only in a moment of need or crisis their importance.

A new light bulb in the bathroom would have perhaps spared his tripping over the half full can of Milwaukee's Best beside the toilet and cracking his head against the tub. That drip in his ceiling, if tended to earlier, might not've progressed across the room and left the pungent smell of mildewed carpet to greet him when he returned after a week-long bender. If he'd seen to the truck when it first started making that Jimi Hendrix feedback sound every time he touched the brakes, maybe it would still be running instead of sitting in a junkyard, twisted around itself, the shape of a big knotty pine discernible in the negative space. And maybe whatsername, the sad-eyed hippie chick, and Layla, his hound, would not have died refusing to make way for the shattering glass and tree branches suddenly violating the truck's interior. Made him think hard about the consequences of his inaction sometimes.

1

Really missed that dog.

But the doorbell, had it been fixed, would never have rung in the first place and that was what he clung to now, squeezing all the comfort he could from it, the fact that he'd not wasted one minute of his life in the impossibly fruitless task of fixing the damn thing.

It wouldn't have rung because Chowder Thompson would not have pressed the button. Chowder would not have wanted Terry to know he was there until it was too late to fetch a weapon.

The road they were exploring seemed not to care for travelers in first class conditions, let alone the undignified fashion he found himself riding in now, hog-tied with a bungee cord and gagged with dirty socks, bouncing defenselessly against the hood of the trunk every time they hit a pot hole, which were legion. There was a deep and widening cut above his left eye. The flow of blood had slowed, but because of those bumps, never stopped. Every few seconds the wound reopened against the ceiling, leaving a touch more stickiness. He imagined the torn flesh around the cut a new set of lips opening compulsively to kiss the car.

His mind was racing now, trying to come up with a way to live long enough to make a better last mistake than the glaring one coming to his mind. He was entitled to more time, more life and more free shit from wherever he could take it.

Maybe there was something he could offer Chowder, if he was ever given the chance to speak again. What could that be? What could a cold man like Chowder Thompson really want from a skid mark like him?

In his desperation he did something he'd never done before in his lazy-ass parasite life. He put his mind to it.

CHAPTER ONE

TERRY

The idea had been Cal's. "We should go to spring break."

Terry snorted. "That's a long way away."

"Well maybe not Mexico or Florida, but we should look for the slutty college girls around here come spring break time."

"There's a couple of problems I see right away with that. One, not many girls around here go to college and two, the type that like to hang around with their tits askew won't come here to do it."

"No, but the ones who do come back here, they're probably pissed about not being able to go for whatever reason. There's bound to be a few hanging around, looking for a party. Could be."

Working on an idea about comely coeds returning home to Spruce, Missouri to release some sexual tension, Terry Hickerson and Cal Dotson had opted to give their usual watering hole, The Gulch, a rest for a week or two. They'd decided to try elsewhere after watching a series of documentaries about exotic locales where the girls had apparently "gone wild." The films were enough to make Terry think, for the first time, that maybe he should've finished high school and gone to college.

Deciding that it was worth a shot, they'd traveled all the way to Joplin and found themselves at one of those nightclubs with the blue neon lighting and expensive sound systems blasting that shitty music kids liked.

The drinks at this nightmare palace were expensive as hell, and there was a policy about different pay rates based on gender, whereas back at The Gulch, drinks were a reasonable price and there was true equality of the sexes. On the other hand, at The Gulch there were never any women south of thirty, unfamiliar with the sad effects of gravity, or likely to recognize the business end of a toothbrush.

They sat at a table in the back corner surveying the scene through their first pitcher of Bud when Cal made a move into a circle of girls who looked like gazelle around the watering hole. Terry noticed him suck in his gut as he closed in. Terry couldn't hear what anyone was saying, but he had a pretty good idea of how it was going. The gazelle stiffened their posture as the gangly lion approached. They huddled closer together then dispersed on some unseen cue leaving for Cal the slowest of their pack to devour. He backed her up against the bar. The girl was round, but young. Her generosity of flesh was still buoyant instead of slack and she looked not entirely put off by her predator. This might be easier than Terry'd thought.

After a few minutes, Cal left the girl at the bar and returned to the table.

"What's the matter? She looked willing."

"Yeah, think you're right, but I'm in no rush. See how this plays out. Fortunes might improve, but it's good to know I've got options."

"You're too picky."

Cal sounded hurt. "No way. I don't want to settle. I don't have to do fat chicks."

"What's wrong with fat chicks?"

"Sometimes I'm just not in the mood for a fat chick."

"Tell you what though, fat girls know how to present themselves. They can wear make up and they tend to smell good too. They put forth a lot more effort than those skinny-pretties you're saving yourself for."

Cal considered that. After a moment he shrugged, "Not in the mood. Maybe later." He looked at Terry, "You're so hot to trot, go for it, her name's Mindy or Cindy or something."

"Nah, that's okay. Think I'll keep my options open."

"Hypocrite."

"Faggot."

As the night wore on, Cal laid his particular brand of charm on a half dozen other college girls without any success. Terry watched his friend's mood sink. "Stuck up college bitches. Think they're such hot shit, but nobody took them to Florida." After a couple of hours' worth of drinking, Cal abruptly snapped to attention when he noticed Cindy or Mindy flirting with another college boy.

And it was decided. She was for him. Cal staggered confidently across the room and simply shoved the young man out of the way. Terry couldn't hear the exchange, but figured the young guy could also see the look in Cindy or Mindy eyes as well as he could, 'cause he didn't give any more than a token objection to Cal's intrusion which Cal waved off with a distracted swipe that barely connected. Cal hooked his arm into whatsername's and they walked out the front door.

Terry guessed he was on his own. Cal could find his own way home.

In the wake of Cal's exit another group of young women came through the front door and Terry's eye snagged on one of them. She was young, but not scary young. Nothing the law would have an opinion on. She came in with friends, but sat alone while the others quickly picked up escorts and dispersed.

Terry couldn't figure it. He was fairly certain she was

attractive; had shoulder length blonde hair. She had high cheekbones and a small bust, nearly delicate, but not. She was dressed in a floral-print skirt and shirt without sleeves. She had slender, firm arms and what looked like a dragon's tail tattoo snaking around her upper arm. She had a look he decided could be wholesome or wild depending on the cast of her eyes. After his money ran out, Terry went to talk.

"What's wrong with you?" hardly slurring at all.

She looked up, surprised. "Excuse me?"

"Why aren't you paired off?" He gestured at the rather sad collection of talent available. "You engaged?" She shook her head. "Is it the clap?" She started to turn away from him. "Wait, I know. You're a born-over-again?"

"Cold."

Terry helped himself to the seat opposite her. "You got a dick in your panties? I saw that in a movie."

She looked at him again, smiling this time. "Oh yeah? I look like a hermaphrodite? Nice."

"I knew there must be a word for it. I bet you intimidate all the boys with your intellect."

"But not you, huh?"

Terry made a face like he'd bit into a lemon and exhaled, flapping his lips. He was aiming for suavely dismissive, but just sounded like a pissed off horse. "Nah, I'm just drunk enough to ask about what makes me curious." He smiled and winked with both eyes. "And seeing you all alone while your ugly friends have a good time makes me curious. So what is it?" He stared intently at her chest for a three count and then resolutely focused on her eyes.

She turned away again, coyly. "If you don't know, I'm not going to tell you."

"What if I can guess?"

"Okay. Three tries."

"You'll have a drink with me?"

"Three tries."

Terry sat down on the stool next to her and put his beer on the table. Up close she had a natural attractiveness that allowed her to flaunt the conventions of beauty. Her body hair was fine and hardly visible, but there was a bush of it under her arms and probably on her legs too. She had an under-washed and earthy scent to her, but it was light and improved the sterile atmosphere of the club. He closed his eyes and put his fingers to his temples in concentration. After a long moment, his eyes popped open and he tried, "Dyke." She shook her head and he smiled. "Good, though you should know that wouldn't have stopped me." Once more he meditated, then, "Cripple of some sort?" Again she said no. Terry shook his head and dropped his hands in his lap. "Ah, hell. They're just afraid of you."

She smiled. "Maybe."

"Well that settles it, I'm your man. I guarantee I'm not afraid. Guess we're having that drink." He rose and extended his hand to her.

"Where are we going?"

"I've got drinks in my truck." He waited a beat. "I spent all my money already." He ran his fingers through his stringy hair and put on his shit-eatingest smile. "What do you want to do?"

"Get out of here."

"Me too."

Cliff was in no mood.

Chowder Thompson was nothing but a new splinter in his asshole and every minute wasted on this rinky-dink, shitkicker operation Cliff felt that sliver push in deeper. Got fidgety.

The backwood badass routine was tired and Chowder's ex-Buc status meant exactly dick back in Memphis, but Bug was also an ex-Buc and Bug thought he saw fortune flash her snatch when Chowder's name had popped up. Bug had sold the Memphis outfit on the benefits of a partnership with his ex-biker pal and they seemed overly impressed with Chowder's independent status – said 'Go feel him out.' Now Cliff was stuck chaperoning the date. If they woke up knocked-up it was Bug gonna hold the grip-end of this stick, and Cliff would have to jump.

As far as Cliff was concerned, independent just meant Mickey Mouse stakes, plus having to deal with a buncha new poor white trash with very little cash money to spend and another entrenched good-old-boy cop-force to cut in. Besides, since when did they negotiate with two-bit, ofay trailer park pimps?

Watching the former bike buddies trade stories, Cliff thought hard about his options. One way or the other, he didn't figure Memphis needed Chowder Thompson or Spruce, Missouri, and if Bug couldn't see that, then Memphis didn't need his ass either.

Play his cards right, Cliff might be able to have Chowder

knock off Bug.

Then maybe Cliff would draw the assignment to deal with Chowder.

The chance to prove his worth like that would be more than an honor. It would be a pleasure.

CHAPTER TWO

CHOWDER

Chowder looked at this puffy version of his old comrade limping along behind him, and had an unpleasant revelation: *I am fucking old.* Bug was giving him a hard-sell, but thought he had the common touch. Chowder'd heard similar offers before. Work with us. Work for us. Let us lease your assets. From Little Rock, Tulsa, Louisville. He hadn't been sold.

But here came Memphis trotting out Bug. Used to look like a flinty Chuck Connors, but now he resembled a twice-fried ham-steak in a new leather jacket and crisp do-rag carefully tied over that scarred old pate. Bug, who'd done three years in Joliet for the Bucs, back when people said Chowder himself looked like Lee Majors' ugly brother, but was now evangelizing some kind of middle-management office job working for criminal K-Mart.

"Shit, we're getting old, y'know?"

"Speak for yourself, Bug."

"Someday sooner than before is all I'm saying. How well

you walking these days, Chowder? Your knee bend more than thirty degrees? Time to get a cushy job, I think."

"So why Memphis?"

Bug shrugged. "Just the way it happened."

"These guys are organized?"

"Like you wouldn't believe."

Chowder's cabin was not on the lake itself, but high up in the hills beyond with a view that included a fat slice of the water. It was less than ten miles from Darlin's, his trailer park brothel, but nearly an hour's drive along the winding, narrow, unpaved roads that snaked through the hills outside Spruce.

Chowder led his two Memphis guests through the front room and out to the back porch that rested upon fifteen- and twenty-five-foot-long stilts dug into the slope below. With all the lights off, the three of them could see for miles and the sounds of the woodland nightlife was spread over the gaps in the conversation like so much padding. The atmosphere was thick with heat and life. Speaking inside it was like moving under water. Everything slowed to the rhythm of the place.

A glow was visible on the horizon and Cliff, his other Tennessee visitor, the skeptic, pointed languidly toward it. "Branson?"

Chowder leaned forward and spat over the railing. "Yeah. Fuckers taking it in hand over fist."

"Don't have to tell me. Least Elvis had the decency to die before he ended up there." Cliff braced his hands on the railing and looked off into the inky black of the Eastern view. Bug sat in a deck chair and lit a cigarette. Chowder rested his tailbone against the railing and the three of them let the bugs and birds feed and fuck as loudly as they would.

Finally Chowder spoke. "How qualified are you to talk to me?"

Cliff turned and looked at Bug coaxing smoke through the filter.

Bug said. "Hey, you know me, man. I wouldn't bring anybody along that was gonna waste your time. Cliff's qualified, trust me."

Chowder didn't take his eyes off of Cliff. "Whatever I say to you, I don't want to have to say it again to somebody else in a month."

Cliff's gaze firmed up. Chowder went on, "If I deal with you, that's it, right?"

Cliff turned away from Chowder and addressed the night. "I speak for Memphis."

The crunch of tires sounded on the gravel driveway out front. "Good. C'mon, entertainment's here."

It started as dancing. The slinky riff of The Cars' "Let the Good Times Roll" pulsed through the cabin, and the girls stood and began to undulate for them. Bug and Cliff broke out their stash.

It brought some wild times to mind, flying with the Bucs all night down back roads cranked and mellowed at the same time, sometimes days straight, then shacking up somewhere with his old lady or one of the eager hangers-on after his old lady started staying home with the kid. He did miss it sometimes, but as much as he hated to admit it, Bug was right, he was getting old.

Steve Miller muscled his way onto the sound system and the scene turned more social. Cliff, Bug and two of the girls mixed hash and pills. They washed it all down with snifters of cognac as the vintage jukebox in the corner played classic rock that stopped cold at 1982. The cabin was Chowder's Presidential Suite, the place he entertained VIPs if it was called for. The wood was dark and the track lighting just enough to keep you from bumping into the furniture. There was a mammoth satellite dish in the front yard, a boat on a trailer in the garage below and the kitchen and bar were kept stocked with the good life, but Chowder never used the place himself.

If either guest was made uncomfortable by Chowder's abstinence or the gruff woman chaperone watching casually from the dark back corner, it didn't show.

After an hour of unwinding, Bug retired with the blonde

to one of the cabin's bedrooms and Cliff took the redhead into another. The juke continued to suggest a party even after those attuned to its ideas had left the room. Chowder stretched, popped his neck, and went to the fridge in the kitchen. He passed by the fancy stuff and selected a Coors.

"Want one?" he said to the third woman.

"No, I'm good." She was thickly muscled like a farm girl with hair dyed black and cut into abrupt bangs and corners above her shoulders. She had heavy bosoms and wide hips and her arms and legs were far from dainty, but she wasn't fat yet. When she stood, her shape was more apparent. She had the athletic build of a wrestler, low and compact, and she bristled with an intensity that made most people uneasy, which is why Chowder always insisted she stay in a corner, out of the way, when she chaperoned.

"You sure?" Chowder gestured toward the shelves of liquor behind the bar. "Gonna be a long night."

"Dad, I'm fine." She stood and stretched, cracking her back and neck and arms before reaching for the Glock in her waistband and tossing it to her father. Chowder checked the action and slipped it into his own jeans before downing his drink.

"What'd you bring, Irm?"

She went out the front door and Chowder drained a second beer in the thirty seconds it took her to return with a pump shotgun. Chowder whistled low. "You look bad ass."

Irma pretended not to hear. "Ready?"

Chowder grabbed another silver bullet and cracked the tab as he headed back across the room. "Let's give 'em another half hour."

Irm looked irritated, but that wasn't unusual. "The fuck are we gonna do for half an hour?"

Chowder sat down in the overstuffed leather recliner and kicked his feet up. "Bitch about your mom."

Assistant State's Attorney Dennis Jordan found himself in a state of sexual excitement listening to the snitch's story. Police corruption, prostitution, drug-running, murder for hire, it was a career-maker if he'd ever heard one.

He took out his note pad and began to write furiously. After a moment the snitch stopped talking. Jordan looked up from his notes.

The snitch wanted his full attention. "Let's talk about my deal."

ASA Jordan looked over the list of names and titles he'd been making: Senator Dennis Jordan, Governor Dennis Jordan, Attorney General Dennis Jordan and circled the last one written down: Sheriff Jimmy Mondale.

"Alright, let's do. What do you want?"

CHAPTER THREE

MONDALE

The information Chowder had given him was that the house way out off of the county road had a lab in the basement. No shit. The shack was straight out of redneck meth-cook central casting. Jimmy Mondale was one for appearances where drug busts were concerned, so when he'd received the tip, he'd gone through all the proper channels and waited for the wheels of justice to grind along and plant a warrant in their hands.

Deputy Musil pulled his cruiser up next to Jimmy's and the window came down. "Bob."

"Jimmy."

"Got it?"

Musil handed the warrant through the open window. Mondale looked it over carefully, not because he was concerned with its legitimacy, but because he was putting off the raid. He had no particular love for Earl Sutter, but he didn't want to bust him either. Far as he knew, Earl was just another poor, out of work, working-man who cooked crank for his own use and to turn a quick buck. Out here, he didn't even have neighbors to be bothered if he blew himself up.

Mondale was just sweeping up Chowder's work-space.

Deputy Townsend, sitting next to him in the front seat, leaned over for a better view. "Looks good, yeah? Ready?" The young deputy's enthusiasm for this part of the job was common, but it rankled Mondale. Townsend had gone to school with Earl Sutter, grew up in the same area, had probably dated the same girls, maybe went to the same parties and social events, but here's how they turned out; Townsend on the side of the angels, and Sutter a shitbird.

Mondale folded it and nodded his head. "Yeah, it's good. Let's do it." He and Townsend got out of the car and Musil parked his own and joined them. He sent the deputies the long way around, through the scrub trees.

When they'd confirmed their positions, he walked up the gravel driveway, past the exposed cinder-block addition, underneath the gutterless overhang, until he stood on the sagging front porch.

He knocked on the door hard and quick and called out. "Earl Sutter, open up. Police."

And listened.

Inside he heard a faint rustle of movement. *C'mon, don't make it worse.* He rapped again and shouted, "Open up, Earl, or I'll have to come on in. Don't be dumb, son. I've got a warrant here."

From behind the door, he heard the sounds of panic setting in. *Shit.*

The doorframe was rotting and gave way easily with the third kick. The house was dark. Gray daylight dripped through chips in the crumbling aluminum-foil shields plastered into the front windows. The corrosive stink of the place made his eyes water, and he paused to let them adjust to the dark. From the back corner of the house he heard the toilet flushing. He followed the sound.

Mondale heard Musil coming through the back door off the kitchen. Before he reached the back of the house, the bathroom door burst open and the blurry shape of Earl Sutter rushed past him, and through Musil's diving tackle. Mondale stepped over his deputy, checking on him with a backward glance. Musil looked up from the floor at him, "I'm fine," he grunted, out of breath, too old at forty-five for this kind of work. "Go on."

Jimmy had three years on him, but was wiry and agile where Bob Musil had put on a pronounced potbelly that made for a rough landing. He followed Sutter through the house and heard the crash of glass breaking from the bedroom ahead of him. He entered the room just in time to watch the mutt jump out the window he'd just thrown a boom box through. Earl's foot caught on the jagged sill and went down hard, but rolled and was already running when he started to rise.

There was no way Jimmy was following him through the window. He saw Townsend come in from the side and tackle Sutter just as he was about to hit a burst of speed. The two men went sprawling in opposite directions and Mondale turned on his heels and reversed course to the kitchen and the back door.

Musil was right behind him as they hobbled gingerly through the broken glass and garbage spilling out of the overturned trash can on the ground. Outside, they found Deputy Townsend straddling Sutter's back, struggling to cuff him. The self-employed redneck was still wiggling, trying to get away, unable to see that it was over, or unable to care, digging his hole deeper as fast as he could.

"Whoa, there, Earl." Mondale called. The man looked at him, his eyes wide and teeth clenched, "C'mon, son, settle down, not helping yourself any." Some of the fight leaked out of Sutter and the wrestling became less frantic.

Townsend clamped the cuffs around one of Earl's wrists and then the other. The young deputy rolled off of his quarry and stood, beaming at the two older policemen. "That was a rush," he said.

Mondale looked at the man on the ground. His ankle

was cut from catching on glass, going through the window, and it was beginning to bleed profusely. Musil was already on it, trying to staunch the flow with a hankie.

Mondale leaned forward, resting his palms on his knee-caps and sucking breaths greedily. He looked at Townsend. "Go get the car. Get him to the hospital." Townsend nodded and took off at a trot for the cruiser.

Earl Sutter spit. "I don't need no hospital."

"You're my responsibility and you're getting that leg looked at."

"I can't afford no fuckin emergency room."

"Hold still, you're making it worse."

"I ain't goin to no hospital, fuck you."

Deputy Musil reached down and slapped the back of Earl's head. "Hey. Shut up. Save it for your lawyer."

"I ain't got a lawyer, fool."

Mondale knelt down to be at eye level with Earl Sutter. "Listen to me, Earl. This is what you need to do. We're arresting you for that lab you got downstairs, okay?"

"Man, I don't know what you're even talkin about."

Musil broke in. "Don't interrupt the sheriff, asshole."

"Earl, what you're going to want to do is call a lawyer, or call a family member to get one for you."

"Man, I –"

"Earl!" Mondale barked. It got his attention. "You're gonna want to have somebody start working on bail for you too. You have anyone you want me to call, let them know you need bail money?"

Earl started shaking his head, "Nobody I know got that kind of money."

"Listen, son, you didn't point any weapons at us and, as far as this little scratch goes, it doesn't have to have been from resisting arrest. We're talking probably a few hundred dollars, Earl, who can I call?"

Earl Sutter just shook his head.

* * *

Jimmy Mondale had been Sheriff of Hamilton County, Missouri for nearly twenty years, and seen some discouraging things, but nothing torpedoed his boner for life like his ex wife's new name on the caller ID on a Friday night. What the woman could want from him now that she'd moved away, moved on, and moved her bowels so well, he couldn't guess.

He looked at the St. Louis area code and steeled himself. He could ignore the ringing phone, but Shirley would talk to him on the answering machine like she knew he was standing there listening, trying to avoid her. She had a way of sensing that sort of thing that only ended up putting him in a defensive posture every time they spoke. He took a deep breath and picked up.

"Hey Shirl."

"Hey Jim, how are you?" As soon as she spoke, her presence was unwelcome, but unavoidable all around him. He smelled the laundry and spray-cleaner scent of her and could feel the warmth of her breath on his neck like she'd never left. He was going to get drunk after this.

"Same as ever. How're you and whatshisname?" He flinched as soon as he said it. Made him sound as petty and spiteful as he was and didn't want to admit.

"We're fine." She wasn't going to rise to his bait. "Have you talked to Eileen lately?"

Shit. What now? Their youngest daughter, Eileen, had taken on a wild streak in high school that hadn't curbed. He'd had to pull some professional strings to smooth over the trouble she'd gotten into in Cedar Rapids her freshman year at Truman State. He hated doing that, trading on his badge for favors, but what was he supposed to do? She was his daughter. "No, I haven't heard from her, why?"

The heavy sigh on her end came through so clear he got a tingle in his trousers and turned sideways to get more comfortable. "We were expecting her yesterday, but she's a no-show and we thought maybe she'd happened your way."

That cooled his semi, but didn't raise alarm. Eileen was an adult and not obligated to alert her parents of her plans. It was rude, but not out of character, for her to blow them off. "You called Liz?" Their other daughter, married to a dull and successful young lawyer and expecting her first child in Kansas City, had little to do with either of them anymore, angry over the dissolution of their marriage, but was still close with her younger sister.

"Yeah, she hasn't heard anything."

"I'll put out the usual feelers, but don't worry, she's probably just found a new boyfriend." He hated the way that sounded as much as he knew Shirley did, but feigning coolness and resignation regarding their children's life choices was the single edge he had on his ex wife.

"That girl is throwing her life away. How can you be okay with that?"

He smiled a tiny bit at her tone. He'd pushed the right button. "Hey, you know it bothers me, the parade of losers she hooks up with, but she's an adult and not obliged to clear her sex life with her parents." God, that sounded awful. He'd probably pushed too hard.

"You're disgusting sometimes, Jim." She was cold and calm now. He'd lost his advantage by rubbing her nose in it. "Let us know if you hear anything."

"Will do," he said to the empty line.

Where was the Wild Turkey?

CHAPTER FOUR

TERRY

They left in his pickup and drove toward the campgrounds, then went to work on the cooler that Terry kept behind the seat. "Wanna hear a chiropractor's pick up line?" She nodded, slurping the foam out of the top of the aluminum beer can. Terry took her hand, then moved his fingers gently up her arm and examined her elbow gingerly. He turned it, traced his fingers down to her wrist and the heel of her palm, and her fingers closed reflexively over his. "What's a joint like this doing in a girl like you?"

Abruptly she coughed and squeezed her eyes shut against the burn of beer leaking out of her right nostril. She dabbed unselfconsciously at it with the back of her hand, "That's awful." But she was smiling. As he tossed her second Stag to her, she said, "I think you should know, I carry pepper spray and a gun."

Terry nodded his head. "Me too. I'm still not scared."

"It kinda freaks out the guys in Kansas City."

"Oh, yeah?"

"Once I pulled it on a guy who thought he was charming, but wasn't. When I showed him my .380 ACP, he thought it was funny until I fired a round at his feet. Pissed himself."

She opened the door and rolled cat-like outside and leaned her back against his pickup, staring at the night sky. Terry exited his own side and looked skyward too. "Alright. Fair warning. 'Course, I piss myself sometimes anyway. It's not the end of things." He cracked his own beverage and took a long pull as he walked around the back end of the truck toward her. "Anything else I should know?"

She tilted her head back as if giving it careful thought. "Well, I don't shave my legs or under my arms."

"No? Well, you've got that kind of light hair. You can get away with it just fine, I bet."

"I could probably hotwire your truck in thirty seconds."

"Bullshit," he said. Then, "Okay. If you can do it I'll shave my legs and under my arms. If you can't then you have to."

"You're on."

Terry opened up the driver's side and the girl got in. "Ready?" She nodded at him and bit her upper lip with her bottom teeth. "Go."

Terry heard a crack and saw her blonde head bend down to look closer at something while he counted out loud. At the five-second mark, the hood of the truck popped and she got out and lifted it up. At twenty seconds she said, "Damn, it's too dark, I can't see shit."

Terry finished the thirty count shaking his head. "Not my problem, girl. I believe you owe me a shave."

"Mmm. We'll see. I could do it no problem in the day time or with a flashlight, though."

"Again, not my problem. You should be more careful, the wagers you make." She came around to join him leaning against the side of the truck and took a deep breath of the cooling night air. Terry took a long look at her and said, "If we're not careful, this fresh air might sober us up, keep us from being foolish."

She drained her can and reached underneath the hem of

her skirt. Then she stepped backward out of a pair of striped panties and tossed them in the back of the pickup. Terry unfastened his belt and pressed her gently against the side of the truck. She reached behind herself into the cab and fished through her bag. Terry lied to her saying, "It's okay. I got a vasectomy."

She kept fishing. "I need something else." Terry nibbled the side of her neck and took her earlobe between his teeth.

"Then get one for me, too."

She reached down between his legs and guided him, raised her left knee and he held it up. When he found a smooth rhythm she let out a deep sigh and dug her nails into his shoulder. When he felt metal against his face he opened his eyes. She was wrapped around him and holding the .380 flush to his cheek. Her eyes were squeezed tight as the rest of her.

The gun got him going, jump-started his pulse, and when she sensed his climax coming she fired three shots straight up, screaming at the top of her lungs while he finished. He nearly collapsed when it was over, but she held him up, still on one foot, still with one arm clutched under his and over his shoulder.

Slowly she uncoiled from top to bottom and when she dropped her knee and he slid free it was she that seemed to need support. They lay down in the truck bed and looked toward other galaxies. Terry reached back over his head and freed more fuel from the cooler, cracking them open one handed and gallantly passing hers before reaching for his own.

He believed it truly was Milwaukee's best.

After a long, silent interval she turned over and draped her thigh across him. When that produced a stir, she climbed on top and with the pistol still grasped in her left hand, she pinned his shoulders to the hard bed of the truck. "My turn," she said.

CHOWDER

When Irm kicked in Cliff's door he rolled out from beneath

the redhead and fell off the side of the bed. The girl gave a yelp and retreated to the opposite corner of the room. Irm heard Cliff fumbling with his clothing, looking for a weapon. She let the shotgun bark and watched the nightstand disappear in a cloud of cordite and a shower of sparks from the lamp. She walked around the corner of the bed and Cliff leapt at her as she rounded the bend. She raised the butt of the gun to meet his chin and he slumped to the floor, unconscious.

Her father followed Bug into the room with the Glock trained between Bug's shoulders. "Dammit, Irm. I said *quiet*. Is he dead?" Irm put the toe of her boot beneath Cliff's shoulder and kicked him onto his back. Cliff groaned.

"No."

"Well, now we gotta carry him. Bug, get his arms."

"What the hell is this, Chowder? We're Bucs. Don't that mean anything to you?"

Bug, barefoot and covered by jockeys and an unbuttoned shirt that hung open to reveal outlaw tattoos that, to Irm, looked more than a little silly, squatted down and scooped up his partner by the armpits. Irm handed Chowder the shotgun and got her elbows locked under Cliff's knees. With a *hmpff* they had lifted the man from Memphis and were taking him out the door.

"C'mon, girls. Put your clothes on and git." The blonde and the redhead hastily draped themselves and carried their unmentionables in their hands as they bumped into each other in the hall way. Irm gestured to the redhead with her chin.

"Keys on the counter. Get back to Darlin's and wait in my trailer. Don't say nothin." They did as they were told. Irm backed out the front door with Cliff and Bug in tow. Chowder was behind them closing up the cabin. Then he went around and opened up the spacious trunk of Cliff's Lincoln.

Bug and Irm dropped Cliff inside and Bug climbed in on top of his partner, half-naked and mumbling. Irm banged his head slamming the trunk. Chowder chuckled. "That was cold."

Irm shrugged and caught the keys Chowder tossed to her. "Nah, cold is gonna be torching this thing before they're dead." She climbed in and started the engine and watched in the rearview as her father got into his pickup and turned his lights on. She cranked the volume on the tune already blaring. *Let's have a party.* Dropping the big car into gear, she tapped on the steering wheel. "Let's do."

Bowling Green seemed far enough out of the way, and they stopped on the outskirts. From inside the trunk, Cliff and Bug could be heard arguing bitterly over the assignation of blame. Chowder slammed the butt of the Glock on the lid and growled, "Shut up." They did.

Irm busied herself emptying the fuel cans from the back of Chowder's truck into the Lincoln's interior. She paused long enough to eject and pocket the Wanda Jackson cassette before draining the last of the gasoline.

Bug was trying to reason with them from inside the trunk, "Chowder, you know I got nothin but respect for you. You're a Buc, man. I'm a Buc. Take that shit seriously."

Cliff caught the scent of the petrol fumes and began to panic. "Oh, fucking whore mother! Listen, you may have the biggest balls out here in butt fuck country, but if you let me die your life will be over. Everybody knows I went to see you."

Chowder leaned in. "I'm counting on that, asshole." He nodded at Irm, who struck a match and lit a cigarette. "Nothing personal fellas."

"No wait, Chowder! Wait!"

Irm flicked the cigarette into the Lincoln's cab and they got back into Chowder's truck. The banging from the inside of the trunk sounded like corn popping and the shouts of the men kept were unified sounds of exertion, the doomed working together to pop the latch, as Chowder wheeled his truck lazily around waiting to witness ignition. Father and daughter stuck their heads out the windows and looked behind them. Chowder counted to ten then said, "You watch too many movies."

"Shut up."

"Here." He handed her a half full bottle of mash. She took it reluctantly and looked around for a fuse. "Hurry the fuck up. They're gonna bust through that trunk."

The trunk did sound like it might give and Chowder thought about how that would look – cold. He didn't like doing this shit, but he knew it would send the right message. Spruce and Hamilton County were off limits. He reached across Irm's lap and popped the glove compartment. From inside, he removed a lacey pair of panties, which he handed over.

Irm's eyebrows arched subtly while she stuffed the frilly nether garments into the mouth of the bottle and let them get good and soaked before pulling one end out and applying the flame from her Zippo. The stink and smoke of burned plastic filled the cab immediately.

"For shit's sake get rid of it already."

She opened the door and positioned herself ten feet from the Lincoln's open door before dashing the bottle against the steering wheel. The car ignited immediately and the force from the blast knocked her back, but she retained her footing.

"Get in."

The shouts from the car became screams and lost all co-ordinated qualities, the pointlessness of their pounding did not seem to matter and the sound of the fire was already beginning to drown them out. Irm had not got the door closed before her father gunned the pickup down the road and they watched the fire grow in the mirrors. An acrid smell made her nostrils twitch and she stuck her palms under her nose. She adjusted the mirror to see herself better. She located the other source of unpleasant odor. The ends of her hair and eyebrows were curled and singed, making her look like a toddler recently acquainted with scissors. "Fuck." She ran her palms over her face and they came back with black marks on them. "Burnt my hair."

"Throw like a girl, too."

MONDALE

The alarm didn't wake him. He'd been awake for more than an hour before it went off. Mondale turned toward the persistent machine and fought the urge to dash it against the wall. He would be mightily hung over in a few hours and hadn't slept well either. The drinking was not working for him.

He'd passed out quickly thanks to the whiskey, but it proved to be temporary paralysis more than true sleep and he'd begun to toss after a couple of hours, his mind racing the way alcohol and caffeine alike tended to cause it to.

He went into the kitchen and made a pot of coffee. He thought about Shirley because after six years, he still couldn't not. When she'd told him about the affair and that she wanted a divorce, he'd done her a favor by popping her in the mouth, thereby absolving any guilty feelings she may have had about leaving him. That fat lip gave her the clarity and resolve to do what she'd been thinking about for years and he didn't stand in her way. He'd never hit her before, and they were both glad he'd done it.

Shirley'd never told anybody and he'd given her a quick divorce and custody of the children. He'd sent child support for a while, though she'd never asked for it, but he'd stopped when she'd tied a new knot with the fella she'd apparently been carrying on with, behind his back, for over a year.

He arrived at the office early and put on a pot of coffee for the guests of the county. Then he got to work filing reports, perusing the state-wide bulletins and returning e-mails. The one from the State Attorney's office included a phone number that he was encouraged to use as soon as possible.

He got up to fetch the coffee and, making his rounds, stopped outside Earl Sutter's cell. Pasty skin drawn too tight over his chin, cheekbones and forehead, he looked ill, but he was alert. He met Mondale's eyes and the sheriff offered him coffee in a paper cup.

Earl seemed about to tell the policeman to fuck off, but his better instincts rallied and he inclined his head just a bit and accepted the cup.

"Sorry, it's gotta be black. We're out of cream and sugar."

Earl Sutter mumbled his thanks and Mondale squatted against the far wall with his own drink. "Earl, you think of anybody I could call for you, yet?"

Earl shook his head.

"Well, look. You're going to be assigned a public defender, and he or she's going to give you council on your options, which are probably not going to sound very good, any of them, but before you sign anything or make a decision, if you want to get in touch with me, I'll give it a listen. I've seen about every way your situation could break from here and I'll shoot you straight if I think it's a good idea or not. And if it happens to be trickier than I thought, then there are a few lawyers around here that owe me a favor or two. They'd be able to walk you through any sticky particulars."

Earl looked skeptical.

"Son, I've got no interest in seeing you over-pay for your foolishness. Call me once you've talked to your lawyer."

Jimmy got up and walked back to his office, re-filling the cup of the drunk in cell four along the way. Sitting back down, he looked at the phone number from the State's Attorney again. He dialed.

CHAPTER FIVE

TERRY

First light was not the gentle pinkish thing Terry remembered from fishing trips as a kid. The metal bed of the truck seemed to ignite instantly with the first touch of sun and the ringing in his ears could've been bullfrogs, beer or blitzkrieg.

When he turned over she was sleeping, curled around her own knees, backside to him. Terry sat up careful not to wake her or further stir the hornets newly nested in his head. He found his pants bunched around his ankles and pulled them up past his knees and over the great general stickiness further north.

Careful as he was, the scrape of the belt buckle on the floor of the truck woke the girl who turned over and looked into his face, not horrified, or angry, but - and it could have been the effects of sleep, alcohol or embarrassment - red faced.

"Breakfast," she said.

"Thinking so."

He reached down to help her up and they climbed into the cab and rolled the windows down. The radio low and the breeze created by motion considerably soothed the ruckus inside Terry's skull.

At a station break, Terry flipped the radio off. "Why haven't I seen you around before?"

"I don't really live here anymore. Been away at school three years now and I don't come back for breaks except this one."

"I don't blame you. Why come back for this one?"

She shrugged. "Seemed about time. I'm graduating soon and then moving away. Kinda wanted to see this place one more time."

"You grew up here?"

"Uh-huh."

"Me too." Terry pulled in to the Come Back Again diner and the girl snorted. "What?" said Terry, "Thought you wanted breakfast."

"I do. Just haven't seen this place in a long time. My dad used to bring me here when I was a kid. Etta Sanderson still run the show?"

"Think so."

She opened the door and hopped out. "Well let's go say 'hey.'"

The diner wasn't quite bustling, but it would be soon. He grabbed a booth while she went to the bathroom. Terry fished a cigarette out of his pocket and lit up. His lips were dry and his tongue felt like sandpaper when he tried to wet them, but he got the nail secured and lit. He closed his eyes and concentrated on the nicotine shiver that slid slowly from his brain. When it reached his fingertips, he opened them and found the menu. He sensed the waitress approach and turned over his coffee cup.

She filled it and turned over the other cup without asking. Then she said, "You know what you want?"

"Always changing."

"I'll give you just a minute." She started to walk away, but turned back and, like an afterthought, asked, "Was that Eileen Mondale came in with you?"

Terry looked up at her. "Huh?"

30

The waitress, a weathered old gal with a reservoir of sex she kept full, smiled, but looked concerned. "The girl you came in with. Looked like one of the Mondale girls, but I haven't seen her for years." A tingle completely separate from the cigarette began to stir in him. "Is that her? Is that the sheriff's daughter?"

Terry smiled when he saw the girl emerge from the bathroom, face splashed and scrubbed. He studied her closely and thought there was something familiar around her eyes. It was a cold thing he'd seen before. In her father. His mouth parted into a grin so wide it threatened to split his poor lips. "I surely do hope so."

CHOWDER

Chowder pulled into the gravel lot of the Come Back Again diner and shut his door quietly. It was closing in on eight in the morning and the place was bustling. Etta Sanderson pointed him toward an empty booth not yet bussed.

"Yes, ma'am." Chowder muttered, but he liked the old broad. A few heads turned as he ambled down the narrow walk way and he got a couple quick nods that turned away again as soon as he met their gaze before turning to fall gingerly into the booth then twisting and bringing his legs underneath the table.

A few seconds later, Etta was clearing the mess from the previous diners and pouring coffee at the same time. "Want me to leave the paper, Chowder?"

"Hell no."

"Know what you want?"

"Just some taters."

She had spritzed the table with bleach water and he held the coffee close to his face to mask the scent. He scalded his tongue with the first sip, then set it down and began to work the knots out of his neck with his fingers.

"Mornin' Sheriff." He heard Etta say two seconds after leaving his breakfast potatoes beside his coffee.

"Mornin' Etta. Just a coffee please."

Chowder looked toward the front where Jimmy Mondale was standing tall and rigid like he was getting his picture took. The sheriff looked around the room that way that cops do. Seeming casual, but not missing anything. When Jimmy spotted Chowder he made his way down to his booth.

"Mornin Chowder."

"Hey, Sheriff."

"Is that Irm sleeping in your truck?"

"Probably."

"You two go fishing?"

"Something like that."

"Here you go, Sheriff." Etta placed a Styrofoam cup on the end of the counter and Jimmy reached over for it. "Say, it's nice to see Eileen back in town."

"Is it?"

"When did she get back?"

"Got me, I haven't seen her yet."

"Well she looks good. Was with a fella, though." Etta rolled her eyes, "You tell her for me - she could do better."

"Thanks, Etta. Keep the change." Jimmy sat down at Chowder's booth.

"Everything go okay?"

Chowder nodded.

"Memphis is still in Tennessee?"

"Some of it's in Kentucky."

"There's a situation come up, concerns you."

Chowder popped some breakfast potatoes in his mouth and packed them into his cheek like hot savory chaw. He sucked the salt out before swallowing the starchy wad and steeled himself for this latest development with a swig of coffee. "What kind of situation?" Mondale gave Chowder an extra moment to prepare, which only made the big man irritated. "Spit it out."

"Assistant State's Attorney."

Chowder's grip on the coffee mug constricted until the handle came off in his fingers. A redness peeked up over the line of his beard until it touched his eyes. "What about him?" he said, holding his breath.

"Got a bug up his ass. Says he's got an informant."

"Bullshit."

"I'll be receiving him this week. In fact, I shouldn't be seen talking with you long."

Chowder dropped the broken china handle on the table before it was reduced to dust in his grip.

Jimmy eased his posture a little. "I'm working on it. Let's go fishing tomorrow. Talk about it then. Just thought you oughtta know up front." He stood back up and knocked on the Formica tabletop. He strolled toward the door and held it open for Irm, who looked her usual sunshiny self. Jimmy smiled at her and Chowder read Irm's lips from across the room. *Lick my cunt.*

Outside, the sheriff glad-handed a couple of citizens in the parking lot, shooting the shit about weather, high school sports, wives and kids. Chowder looked around the diner at the customers, thinking how much damage he could do taking a fall. Mondale had to be nervous. Their fates were intertwined. His precious little community would crucify him if they knew what kinds of things their bland and easy-going Sheriff Mondale was up to, running dope and whores, killing off the competition. Chowder and the sheriff had consolidated and regulated all the narcotics traffic in Hamilton County over the past ten years and it had not been done with a kind word. Ask Bug. The price of keeping independent was one they had and would continue to pay together. The lawman had to be making his BVDs damp at the thought of some loud-mouth speaking to a State's Attorney. He had as much to lose as Chowder did. Yeah, he was nervous.

Through the window, he watched Mondale climb into his cruiser and smile at some Christian folk pulling in for breakfast. Chowder admired the sheriff's cool as he gripped his mangled coffee mug and took a sip.

Irm was wiping the corners of her mouth with her palm when she sat down opposite him. Her face was still smudged black in spots and the burnt ends of her hair stood straight up like tiny antennas on her head. "Why didn't you wake me up?"

"You're grumpy when you wake up."

"Fuck you. You talk to the sheriff?"

"Uh-huh."

"I don't like it. You can't trust the police."

Chowder leveled his eyes at his daughter's until she looked away. "You trust me?"

Irm just nodded.

"Then shut the fuck up."

She scowled and picked up a menu.

Chowder pushed his plate toward her. "Have some taters."

CHAPTER SIX

MONDALE

"Hello?"

"Hey Shirl, it's me."

"Jim, what is it?"

"It's about 'Leen."

"Oh my god, what is it, Jimmy?"

"Relax, she's in town."

"Jesus, Jim, don't ever start a sentence that way. I thought —"

"I know, I'm sorry, just thought you'd want to know as soon as I did."

"She's staying with you?"

"No, I haven't seen her, but Etta Sanderson spotted her at the diner."

"That child."

"Yeah."

"Thanks for calling, Jim. If you see her, tell her…"

"Will do." Jimmy hung up the phone and turned on the light to see his daughter better. She sat on his couch flipping the channels on his television and drinking his beer.

"Hi, Daddy. I brought the car back."

The night before, he'd come home to find his civilian car gone. After Etta Sanderson mentioned seeing her earlier, Eileen, as the thief, made sense. "Hey, hon." He walked behind her, bent over the couch and kissed the top of her head. It smelled like patchouli and cigarettes. "When'd you get to town?"

"Couple days ago. Was that mom on the phone?"

"Said she'd been expecting you."

"Huh. You talked to Etta?"

"Most days. You know, if she hadn't told me she'd seen you, I would've put out an APB on my car."

"Sorry. I needed to borrow it. She's the best."

Jimmy went to his bedroom and began to undress. He called to the next room. "You know I don't mind you borrowing it, but I need a heads-up next time."

"Sorry, I just figured you had the other, too. Filled the tank before I brought it back."

"How long you fixin to stay?"

"I just came by to say 'hey.' I'm staying with a friend."

"Etta said you had a boy with you."

"Maybe, but that's not my friend."

"Oh? Who is he?" He was down to his shorts and white t-shirt and picking up his socks from the bedroom floor to deposit in a pile in the bathroom when she came to the door.

"Nice try. Nobody. I'm staying with Julie Sykes."

"From school?"

"Yeah, why?"

"Nothin, I just didn't think you kept up with anybody from school."

"I don't. I just ran into her and she said I could stay over."

"Huh. What's she up to these days?"

Eileen shrugged. "She teaches school. I'm going back tomorrow. Figured I'd come see you."

"Lemme get cleaned up, we'll grab some dinner." Jimmy shut the bathroom door and stripped. He turned on the shower and placed his face into the stream as quickly as possible. He wasn't crying. Not even close.

Eileen sat across from him in the booth just like she'd done as a young girl when he'd treat her and her sister to milkshakes after a movie or a ride in his cruiser. She sat there looking, for all the world, like her mother and his own flesh, but also something alien. Something he couldn't begin to guess at. He wondered at her.

She pushed up the sleeves of her shirt and he caught sight of a tattoo on the underside of her forearm. She caught him staring and pushed the sleeve up all the way so he could see it clearly. Some kind of twisting of wire or vine or some such neo-pagan imagery.

"Like it?"

"No."

She pretended to be hurt. "You probably wouldn't like the rest either."

Mondale smiled into his drink. He wouldn't take the bait that easy. "Think about calling your mom?"

"Not really."

"She's concerned, you know."

Eileen shrugged, then produced a cigarette. She placed it between her lips, and, as an afterthought, offered the pack to her father.

He hesitated, then reached to take one. Share what you can with your daughter, he reasoned. She lit his and then her own and they both pushed their plates toward the middle of the table and regarded each other while tasting the first of their after-dinner smokes.

Etta Sanderson cleared their plates and Eileen called out for her to join them. Etta glanced over her shoulder and said she would in a minute. "How about Elizabeth? Talked to her lately?"

Eileen nodded, exhaling a blue plume, "Yeah, Liz is good. I can't believe I'm going to be an auntie. I'm gonna teach that kid so many bad habits." They both smiled and Mondale left his cigarette in the ashtray as Etta returned and sat down next to him across from Eileen. Etta reached for his cigarette, took a quick drag, replaced it and grabbed Eileen's hand.

"You ready to go back, girl?"

"Uh-huh. Study, study, study."

"Oh, it makes me so happy to see you doing good. Honey, you make sure to call your momma too. She'll want to talk to you." Eileen smiled sadly at Etta. "I know how it is with mothers. And daughters. And granddaughters. You know Cyndi's about to have her first?"

Eileen lit up and squeezed Etta's hand. "Really? That's great. You're going to be a great-grandmother, that's so sweet."

Etta recoiled playfully. "Don't go calling me great grand-mamma. No call for that." Etta stood and so did Eileen. They hugged and Etta returned to her shift. Eileen watched the woman work.

"Any thoughts about what you'll do after graduating?"

Eileen looked at her father again. "Not really."

Mondale reached for the smoldering cigarette in the ash-tray. He knocked the ash loose and took a drag. "Ever think of coming back here?"

Eileen gave a low snort. "No."

"I could get you some work down at the station."

"Are you serious? You think I wanna monitor a radio or make sandwiches for prisoners? Really?"

Mondale's turn to shrug. "It's a thought. It's a job. Might give you some perspective, some space to make your next move from."

"No offense, Dad, but that kinda sounds like hell."

"Think about it." He ground out the cigarette and reached for the check. "I'll leave the offer on the table."

He brought Eileen back to his house and they sat on the front porch, lighting another pair of cigarettes. The dark was thick, as was the sound of nocturnal communities of the wild. Eileen said she had to pee and went inside, leaving him alone. He took a deep drag and hit that light-headed spot he was looking for. He sat absolutely motionless and thoughtless till she returned three minutes later, cracking the seal on a fifth of bourbon. She handed him a coffee mug and filled it to the top before doing the same to her own.

He sipped at it, grimaced to let the liquid shoot to the back of his gums and sting before swallowing. He'd quit smoking years ago for reasons he was having a hard time recalling, and the mixture of alcohol and nicotine was potent, though he was guarded against it in the presence of his child.

"What happened to you, Dad?"

He wasn't sure she'd actually spoken for a moment. "What do you mean?" He didn't think he was up for this.

"I mean, when did you get so sad?"

He choked on his drink. "That how you see me?"

"That's how you are."

"Well, I'm not so sure about that." He coughed again, and reached for a new cigarette. "But maybe just having you around is reminding me of sad things." He waited for a response, but none came. "Like maybe I miss having a family."

"You really hit mom?"

He nodded. "She tell you that?"

Eileen shook her head. "Didn't see it coming?"

He shrugged. "I'm not sure. At the time, I would've said 'no,' but now…" The thought faded and nobody tried to revive it. After some silence he turned to face her. He smiled. "I'm glad you came to see me. I miss you and your sister." She tried to smile back, but it was a discouraging sight so he looked away toward the tree line. "And your mother. I miss her too."

The dark shapes of the trees sure were interesting. "I know I wasn't much good at it, but I enjoyed being a father like you wouldn't believe."

Eileen coughed and smiled. "Yeah, maybe I don't believe it." She killed her drink and poured another. "But what do I know?"

"So what about you, then?"

"What happened to me?"

He nodded.

"Let's pretend I don't know what you mean. You're going to have to say it."

"Alright. When did my sweet, bright little girl…" Her face stiffened into half-defiance, half-provocation that way that young children's and teenagers' do. That look that says they hate you for pushing so far into them and that they want you to do it all the same. He knew he wasn't up to it. He looked away again into the night. "Never mind."

A pair of headlights cut through the yard and aimed at the house. Jimmy shaded his eyes as the car pulled into his driveway. He was aware of Eileen's unwavering gaze on the back of his head and when the headlights died, he turned to look at his girl. Her eyes were wet just a little, but the rest of her had hardened and set. She collected her cigarettes and their cups. Rising to go inside, under her breath she said, "Fuck you."

The car door opened as the screen door closed and a young woman Eileen's age, Julie he guessed, got out. "Sheriff Mondale," she greeted him.

"That you, Julie?"

"Yeah, it's been a long time."

"Sure has." He was trying to recall her face from the past. All those school-girls had been the same. None so special or noticeable as his own. But now that he looked close, he thought he did remember the way her nose pointed to the right and the lopsided quality it gave her face. Especially when she smiled. Yeah, Julie, she was a cutie, he had to admit.

Eileen came back out of the house with a bag of laundry she'd done while he was at work. She kissed her fingertips and touched the back of his head as she walked by him. "See ya, dad." She passed her friend and climbed into the passenger's side of the waiting car.

Julie smiled at him and waved. A dimple appeared in her right cheek and the tilting of her head toward the side with all the distinguishing features made it seem all the weight inside her head had shifted over there. "Good to see you again,

Jimmy."

He smiled back at her and said, "You too, sweetheart." As the girls drove away he felt a pinch of a disturbing nature in his belly. The way she'd looked at him and the easy, familiar way she'd spoken to him was pleasing, he couldn't deny.

"Jimmy, huh?" he addressed himself, "You're a dirty old man."

TERRY

Terry had done thirty days in County once for a collection of unpaid fines. He figured it was easier to do the time than pay the money. He spent it reading the funny pages, playing hoops and doing lots of push-ups. There was a Mex named Estrada sharing his cell. Terry called him Ponch. Ponch wrote letters non-stop.

"I knew Mex's had lots of kids, but damn, how much family you got, Ponch?"

His celly shrugged. "This is no family correspondence. I'm a published writer."

"The fuck out."

"No shit, *gringo*. You've probably read some of my work before."

"I look like a reader to you?"

Estrada marked off his accomplishments on the fingers of his right hand. "I've been published in *Leg Show, Swank, Black Tail* and even *The Forum*."

"*Penthouse?*"

"*Hot Talk* too. You wanna shake my hand now, *pendejo?*"

Terry was fascinated and urged him to recount each published letter he could remember. Over the next few weeks, Terry and Estrada wrote sixteen letters collaboratively including one eventually placed in an erotic anthology with stories that featured non-traditional participants. Their piece was a first-person account of a teenaged blonde with more natural sex-drive than the men in her town seemed capable of handling. She'd taken a journey across the country from Tucson to Tallahassee, to find fulfillment in the hands and at the feet of other erotic sojourners including a family of midgets and blind co-joined twins. Ponch told him that the American prison system was full of writers like himself and that the Russians didn't have a corner on the incarcerated author market. Terry had entertained the idea of continuing to write when he was released, but found that the discipline was beyond him.

How had the sheriff, walking around with the broom snapped off up his butt, wound up with such wild offspring? Terry had his suspicions that he was merely playing a role in a carefully constructed 'get fucked' lifestyle that she would flaunt anytime the old man tried to have sway in her life, but far from minding, he marveled at the symmetry that their independent plans were so intertwined and reliant upon the other suddenly.

He sat behind his dad's old typewriter and tried to channel Estrada. He'd written down the bones without changing the truth, but found he lacked the Mexican's knack for words and was powerfully discouraged until he decided to include his revenge angle. Then he found that the passion flowed effortlessly and that the real erotic charge had been hiding beneath the motive, and not the cold mechanics, of her degradation.

Terry's home-cooked connection, Earl Sutter, was out of business and probably not going to be seen for years, if ever again. Terry took that personal. Forced him to buy from Chowder Thompson, and Terry didn't like supporting big business on principal.

So he did his part. Wrote his heart out and defiled the sheriff's daughter in fiction and in ways at least inspired by the last few days, if not strictly factual. Kicker was, she'd probably dig it if she read it. Mondale's little girl. Who'd have thought?

By morning he believed it was ready to send out.

Terry pulled up to the house Cal Dotson shared with his great aunt Jeannette all revving engine and squealing brakes.

He blared the horn instead of pulling donuts on the lawn like he wanted to. After a ten second blast, Cal's neighbor opened his door and shouted at him to knock it off.

"Make me," countered Terry.

The skinny guy with the heavy stubble and stubborn patch of black hair dug in atop his head, where all others had long ago fled, closed his door behind him and started walking toward Terry who turned up the truck's radio. *Rock 'n roll ain't noise pollution.* He revved the engine and got ready to dance.

The neighbor picked up an abandoned rake, leaning against his front porch and gripped it like a bat. Terry made a show of rolling up his window and slapping down the lock, but when the neighbor was within striking distance of the Chevrolet's door, Terry whipped it open and caught the man in the kneecap.

The neighbor dropped to the ground clutching his leg to his chest and Terry jumped out of his truck and kicked him in the kidneys.

"Hey asshole, why don't you make me, huh? Why don't you fuckin make me, asshole? Make me, faggot." The man yelled and Terry used his boot to snap his jaw shut, and the sharp click of his teeth excited him. The swallowed yell turned into a groan then into a low sob.

Cal Dotson's door finally opened and his friend emerged with a rolled up magazine in one hand and a chicken drumstick in the other. He had apparently been in the commode. "Hoah, lookit who it is!"

Terry quit stomping the neighbor and turned to Cal coming outside. The neighbor groaned, tried and failed to stand. "Come on, we'll hit Darlin's."

Cal went back for his good shirt and Terry sat in the car. The neighbor's door opened again and a small boy wearing a t-shirt of karate turtles came out to their wooden porch and stood looking at Terry who lit a cigarette and winked at him. The boy looked at his father lying on the lawn and back at Terry who raised his eyebrows.

"You gonna do something about it?" he said under his

43

breath from behind the glass.

The boy searched the lawn carefully to take in the whole story before making any rash decisions. His eyes lingered on the rake beside the prone figure of his father. Terry smiled. *Go for it.* But the kid was smarter than that.

Cal came back out wearing a collared shirt only slightly too small for him and ignoring the objections his great aunt was dishing out while locking up the house. He did pause in front of the car though.

"What?" said Terry.

"Help me out." He was stooping to grab his neighbor under the arms to support him. "C'mon, Jeanette'll think it's me and call an ambulance or something."

"Oh for fuck's sake." But he got out and helped.

Cal continued. "One time she called information for the number of some emergency room rummy who'd glued her skin back together. Remember when she slipped off the toilet and sliced her shin on that metal magazine rack she kept in there? Her skin was so thin, the doc said he couldn't stitch it, so he glued it shut?"

Terry didn't remember, but helped Cal drag the man back to his porch where he mussed the little boy's hair. "Yeah, she ran that phone bill way the fuck up explaining to the Indian lady on the other end that her skin was like tissue paper. So, yeah, that's when I took the batteries out of the mobile and re-installed that rotary in her room. She can't keep a train of thought long enough to dial a number with that thing, but I'll tell you what, that doctor's saved me a whole lotta bill dodging. I ain't been to the emergency room with her since. You gotta look for the stuff that says 'non-toxic' which means it's no good for anything else, but it holds old ladies together okay. I bet if you was to make all the glue and duct tape on that old bat suddenly disappear, she'd fall apart a second later."

The kid glared at Terry after helping his father lower himself gently to a seated position. Terry winked.

* * *

When they were on the road, Cal said, "Where the shit you been? You know I nearly got took last week at this mom n pop I hit in Neosho. Son of a bitch come at me with a knife. Surprised the shit outta me. Lookidit." Cal pulled up his shirt revealing three angry red marks pocking the otherwise immaculate pale, doughy expanse of his torso. Sure enough, there was a clear gel crust covering all three and flaking at the edges. "Stabbed me."

Terry squinted at his glue-lacquered wounds. "Over a couple hundred bucks? The fuck out."

I'm telling you, man, I needed my partner. Watch my back." Cal scratched at some of the flaking glue on his belly. "Yeah, everybody's getting touchy about their money."

"Well, I'm back."

"Fuckin A. From where though?"

"I been around."

Cal pulled his shirt down. "Doin what? Nobody's seen you since spring break."

"Affairs of the heart."

"You sly dog. Who is it been squeezing your lemon?"

Terry leaned over and whispered salaciously, "Just take a wild guess."

When they pulled into the lot, both were grinning stupidly and Cal was shaking his head. Terry'd been telling the tale of his time with the sheriff's daughter and his decision to chronicle it with an eye toward publication.

"You wrote it all down? What if the sheriff has a gander at that?"

"I hope he does and everybody else too."

"You're my hero, man."

"You heard about Earl Sutter, right?"

Cal nodded solemnly. "Took his house. He's going away for a long time."

"And over what? Chickenshit cook charge."

"Intent."

"Fuckin A, man. He was my sometime hookup, too."

"Didn't make him rich, did it?"

"Fuckin movies got it wrong. So fuck the po-lice."

Cal smiled. "Fuck their daughters anyway."

As devout and dedicated as they were to the philosophy and discipline of always having a good time, Terry noticed that more often than not, the two of them were likely to clear a party out. The social circle around the eternal pit-fire out front of Darlin's was crowded when they arrived, but after two quick beers all the johns had moved on save one stubborn old fucker Terry'd seen there before, leaving Terry and Cal the run of the suddenly available stock.

Terry hosted a pudgy girl with wide hips and flesh spilling out every gap in her clothing, on his lap. He made her to be twenty, as she looked to be in the neighborhood of thirty. She pushed her chest into his chin and it reeked of five-dollar perfume, but smelled better than most other things in his life. He whispered into her cleavage. "What's your name, girl?"

"Cinnamon," she cooed, pressing his face deep into her gland canyon. "Call me Cinnamon, sugar."

"What if I wanna take you to dinner, Cinnamon? What would I call you then?"

"You can't afford to buy me dinner, sugar."

What did that mean?

Irm Thompson came out of one of the trailers just then. She caught Terry's eye and he called out to her. "Hey, I'm kindly needin some big girls tonight. You interested?"

Irm bristled as she passed, muttered, "Lick my cunt, shitbird."

He called to her retreating backside. "Take you up on that, sweetie." He had an appetite this night. He wasn't interested in one of the stick-girls that looked like they might snap in two beneath him. He thought he'd need every inch and pound of Cinnamon to satisfy him. Recounting his exploits with Eileen Mondale for Cal, after kicking on the neighbor, had stoked a heat inside him. Not yet a flame, but he could tell it was going to burn bright and hot tonight and he wanted to build up to it proper. Cracking his third silver bullet he turned to the gnarly geezer.

"You sure are one horny old toad, huh? Waitin for that turtle to come out of its shell?"

The old man wore dingy, once-blue jeans so big on him a new hole'd had to be poked in the leather belt that was cinched up near his armpits. He had a J.B. Hunt ball cap high up on his forehead with long, stringy strands of gray hair poking out the back and he didn't acknowledge Terry, but kept on staring into the fire, throwing in a plastic bottle now, a pine cone later.

Cal was having difficulty deciding who, among the professionals, to invest his great aunt's government check in. He sought guidance from his friend. "What do you think, tonight? I can't say blonde ever gets old, but y'know there is something a little dangerous about red."

"So get both. What kind of cheap bastard are you?"

"Yeah, I like Vanilla and I like Strawberry and I sure as shit like Chocolate, but I don't truck with Neapolitan. It don't seem right."

"First time I heard you use that logic to talk yourself out of a thing." Terry turned to the old-timer, "What do you think?"

This time the geezer did speak, but he never looked out of the flames. "I think you talk too much."

This brought a laugh from Cal. "You got his number, mister." He turned to Terry. "He's got your number."

Terry admired with his hands the soft roll of skin exploding out between the top of Cinnamon's jean shorts and beneath her blouse knotted at the midriff. He clutched two handfuls. "The hell you say?"

The elder poked a blackened pop can in the fire with a long stick and ignored Terry completely. Terry snaked one of his hands into Cinnamon's jean shorts, but quickly ran out of room to maneuver. He sat there with his hand stuck and turned toward the ancient mariner. "I asked, 'the hell did you say?'"

The old-timer turned and looked at him like a mirror, the way his son Wendell did when Terry could establish eye contact. Terry felt punched. It charged the moment in another fashion that he was not crazy about. When the man spoke, his gums rubbed together and made Terry want to plead with him to stop. "I said you talk too much. You think anybody likes to hear you talk? You think anybody likes you period? You think you got a reason to live? Shut the hell up."

Cinnamon gave a grunt, the beginning and end of a short-lived bout of indignation, as she was ejected from Terry's lap. Terry leaned forward, elbows on his knees, and gave the old-timer his full attention.

"Do you know me? Think you dish out the wisdom of the ages?"

Cal had put his important decision aside for a moment, watching the exchange with great interest.

"What's a shriveled up piece like you do here other than burn trash and scare off the young girls?" Terry stood before the old man who leaned his head sharply to his right in order to look around Terry's legs at the demise of a plastic bottle he'd pitched atop the fire. "Hey, old-timer, ain't you got kids or descendents or something to spend your money on?"

"Nah, fuck that." The geezer was trying to see the fire that Terry was crouched in front of. "Move out the way. I can't see."

Terry moved as best he could to block whatever the old-timer was staring at and received a sharp knock on the side of his knee from a stick the elder held in his fist. Terry yelped and hopped out of range of the stick. He came down clutching his knee.

Cal guffawed and Cinnamon covered her mouth, chuckling. Terry stood firmly on one foot and extended the other, kicking the old man's chair over backward. Cal laughed harder, but Cinnamon gasped and rushed over to the old man's aid. The old-timer was like a turtle on its back, unable to roll onto his side because of the chair's arms.

When he was back on his feet, there was fire in the man's eyes.

"Anything more to add?" asked Terry, fairly certain there wasn't.

This time, the old man's stick jutted straight into Terry's stomach and knocked the wind out of him. He clutched his midsection and doubled over without any breath to curse the geezer with.

The old man turned and ran, which was more like a shuffle, and disappeared into the nearest covering of trees. Terry stumbled after him a couple of steps before stopping to rest his hands on his knees and pant.

Cal decided on red.

CHOWDER

From inside the trailer that served as Darlin's office, Chowder watched the circle of regulars sitting around the bonfire outside. He was going over the receipts with Tate Dill. The skinny little shitheel was the closest thing to a manager he had to leave in charge if he ever left town. He was supposed to be training Irm to run all the businesses, but outside of muscle work, she'd shown little aptitude for it.

Behind him, Tate sat at the desk completing a customer transaction. "Can I get a copy of the receipt?" asked the man. Chowder turned around and watched Tate print one up, tear it off and hand it to him. Ed Castro was a harmless guy. Fifty years old, six foot one, two-forty-five, grey where there was any left up top. He wore glasses and plaid shirts beneath pressed coveralls and a ball cap creased in the middle, which recommended Chowder's Bait 'N More.

Chowder leaned against the wall and asked him, "What's that for?"

Ed shrugged. "Always get receipts. Just a habit, I guess."

Chowder held out his hand, "Lemme see it."

Ed looked at Tate, then fished it out of his pocket, which was littered with crumpled souvenirs of the day's transactions.

He dropped a reminder he'd spent twenty-three dollars on gasoline and a keepsake from the Come Back Again with a personal note from the waitress, Jackie, telling him to 'have a good day' and signed with a heart in place of the dot above the "i" in her name.

Chowder looked at the receipt just issued for fifty dollars worth of live bait and Coors Light from Chowder's Bait 'N More. "What's your business, Ed?"

"Pardon?" asked Ed, a little uncomfortable being under Chowder Thompson's microscope.

"What do you do for a living?"

"Jeez, Chowder, you know I got the grocery."

"Uh-huh. You carry beer at your place?"

"Yeah."

"Imports and shit?"

Ed looked to Tate for help. He was confused. Tate had nothing. "Not really. Not much."

"Coors Light? You carry that one?"

"Sure. Of course."

"Then what the fuck do you need to be buying it from me for?" Chowder handed the receipt to the big man to inspect.

"Uhhh."

Chowder crumpled the receipt and tossed it into the trash can. "You show your wife those receipts?"

Ed Castro's face turned red. "Of course not."

"Well, I hope not, Ed. Seems that might be the kind of thing that's tricky to explain."

"Yeah, guess so."

Chowder turned to Tate. "No more receipts for customers. Some genius's gonna try and deduct a blow job from their taxes." Ed Castro looked at Tate.

Tate winked. "You wouldn't do that would you, Ed?"

Ed stammered. "Huh? No. 'Course not. Hey."

Chowder turned his attention back to the fire outside while Tate reassured Ed Castro that he was a valued customer and ushered him out the door. In the lot a Chevy truck pulled in. There was a cramp in his gut. Maybe he was getting an ulcer.

Chowder sat on the commode with a book trying to coax his stubborn bowels into some kind of truce. This sort of sneak attack worked sometimes. If he sat long enough, relaxed and concentrating on something entirely other, he might produce, but at the moment he was accomplishing exactly nothing.

The door shook with a sudden pounding and Tate's frantic voice shouting, "Chowder, you better come see!"

He clenched his sphincter tight and knew it would take a professional safe cracker to open it again. His anger rose quick. "Get out!"

"Sorry Chowder, but you're gonna need to come out here quick."

"The hell, Tate?"

"Irm's gonna kill him."

He dropped his book and wiggled his jeans over his hips. He looped his belt and smacked Tate with the door when he flung it open. Tate just pointed to the window. Chowder went to it and parted the Venetian blinds. Tate was right. Irm looked like she might kill the shitbird bleeding all over the side of the trailer. Had the guy pinned against the aluminum side with her left forearm and was hitting his face repeatedly with her right. After a blow, which left a tooth embedded between her knuckles, she let him drop to the ground and began kicking his ribs in.

Chowder looked at Tate and saw the beginning of a rising welt above his right eye. Chowder guessed it was from trying to interfere with Irm's whuppin and not from getting hit by the bathroom door. "Told ya."

The front door crashed open and Chowder stepped out and across the lot in five seconds. He roped his arm around Irm's midsection and she screamed and struggled as he picked her up off of the unconscious man. Chowder caught an elbow on the side of his head for his efforts and threw her against the wall of the trailer.

With a yell of frustration, Irm launched off the dented aluminum back toward the man on the ground and Chowder put her down with a right to the left side of her head. His daughter was out immediately and farted loudly as the tension melted out of her. She looked fifteen years younger instantly. He saw her round-faced and chubby, wearing purple tights and a hooded sweatshirt in the principal's office, sitting in the chair, sullenly swinging her feet while the flustered educator recalled the list of injuries she'd inflicted on boys during the school year.

"I'm afraid young Irma has exhausted the last of our good graces, Mr. Thompson. She has no respect for the authority of faculty or the right of her classmates to an education."

He'd taken her for a root beer on the way home while he thought on it, trying to predict her mother's reaction to the news she'd been ejected from school again. Irm had picked her nose and wiped her fingers on the underside of the table, unflinching beneath his gaze while he killed a pot of coffee. Neither had said a thing the whole time.

"Grab her up top." He said to nobody. Tate came around and reached under her armpits while Chowder got her knees. They hefted her into the office and laid her on the couch. Her left eye was beginning to blow up and turn purple. Tate went to the kitchenette and began filling a Ziploc baggie with ice cubes. "What're you doing?" asked Chowder.

"Just getting her some ice," Tate said, "For the swelling."

"Uh-uh. Let that shit swell. Her pageant days are behind her anyhow."

The sound of a truck pulling quickly out of the lot sent him to the window again. That rusty Chevy was gone, leaving a cloud of exhaust. Great. His chicken-dick buddy had split. He went back outside to check the damage.

There was a semi-circle of spectators around the bloody guy on the ground. Some of them glanced in the direction of the departing car. "What happened?" Chowder demanded.

The chunky new girl, Cinnamon, spoke up. "He provoked her."

Chowder looked down at the victim and saw that it was Terry Hickerson.

"Shit," he muttered. No doubt he did. "How exactly did he do that?"

Cinnamon giggled a bit at the memory. "He was real worked up all night. Just all riled. Kept after folks till, I don't know, they hit him." She shrugged like he was a puzzle. "Offered Irm twenty bucks to go three ways with us."

"That's all?"

Cinnamon nodded. "He had a way, though. You had to be there, I guess."

Chowder patted Terry's pockets and retrieved his wallet. Inside, he found three credit cards, none with names matching Terry's, a couple old lotto tickets and a note written in magic marker.

Chowder unfolded it and saw a phone number written beneath the announcement that if you have found this note on the unconscious body of Terry Hickerson you were advised to call his son Wendell Hickerson, who would come pick him up.

"You gotta be kidding me."

CHAPTER SEVEN

TERRY

Terry Hickerson's house had been constructed much like his life had been - with many odd bits strung together in unlikely juxtaposition, blaspheming symmetry and patched on as afterthoughts years in between inspirations.

The original structure consisted of a small bedroom and bath with a kitchen and living room heated by a wood-burning stove, simple and executed with enough integrity to bear the years and indignities they carried without a creak. A door had been cut into the bedroom and another, larger bedroom and bath added on so that reaching them required passing through the front. The addition was not heated and thus unused during the coldest months. It leaked in the northwest corner during the constant showers of spring and late summer.

A canopy had been erected on the house's east side and converted later into a single car garage. Eventually, this was the new, improved kitchen with cabinets on the back wall and linoleum tile on the floor. Somewhere along the way, enthusiasm for this project had waned and the south wall was never completed, leaving the barn-style doors, added when it was a garage, until they broke completely off the rusted hinges. Now there was a vinyl tarp fastened across, which whipped about in the winds strong enough to penetrate the woods, and required replacing every two years. The room's function had returned to garage, though not the type used to shelter automobiles, only tools, scrap wood for the stove or for patching holes, paint cans and sundry broken things awaiting repair or salvage.

Each addition, over the years, had begun to sink into the soft earth of the yard, leaving varying degrees of incline toward the original modest square structure and daylight gaps in portions of the ceiling that were covered eventually by plywood pieces which had formed, by providence, to the same approximate size and shape.

With his parents separated Wendell Hickerson had split time between them by season once he'd started school. During the winter and spring he lived with his mother in the house she'd moved into just before Wendell's first birthday. At the last bell of every school year he'd take up residence in the back room of his father's shack.

The morning of Terry's eviction from Darlin's, thirteen-year-old Wendell had taken him back to his home, but been unable to move him out of the car and so left him to sleep it off in the back of his mother's station wagon, parked in the shade of the long, dirt front drive. The trees surrounding the house provided the only shelter from the summer heat and served to obscure the dwelling almost completely from the pig-trail it was serviced by. In effect, it was more a cave than a building and passers by, were there ever any, might puzzle over the mailbox standing alone on the side of the road.

Layla, his father's terrier mutt, nuzzled him insistently when he'd settled into the cracked pleather recliner in front of the squat stove. He'd grabbed a beer from the cold box and cracked it with his left hand while giving Layla her requested thumps with his right. Satisfied, she'd returned to her place on the couch and stared at him while drifting in and out of sleep. When he'd finished the first, Wendell gave a moment's pause before opting for a second beer. The school day, he'd decided, was already a loss. His mom was going to be pissed, but that was nothing new.

He'd taken her car before. Just meant she had to walk or get a ride to work. She'd get over it soon enough. She'd be a lot more worked up if he brought it back with Terry sleeping inside. After the second he sucked down a third and settled in for a nap.

He woke two hours later to Terry smacking him on the side of the head. "Just go on and help your own self, then. Just go on and take my last beers, why not?" His father seemed upset regardless of the obvious moral low-ground. As if he weren't beat to shit by a girl and banned for life from Darlin's.

Wendell didn't say anything, but got out of the seat and relocated to the spot Layla had napped in. She trotted happily through the room, excited to have the whole gang together. She licked Wendell's dangling hand and went back to Terry's side and awaited whatever great idea he would have about what they should all do.

"Chowder says you shouldn't go back." Wendell offered, hoping to inspire some sheepishness on his father's part. Remind him of the morning's circumstances and why his face was slurpy-colored and his mouth lips looked like pussy lips – all weird shades of flesh and not quite made to close right – and why Wendell was over there and not at school in the first place. Plus where was his tooth?

"That so?" said Terry, settling on a grape Vess that he kept in the cold box for mixing drinks, if he happened to bring that type of woman home. "Well, Chowder Thompson can lick my nuts. This is a free country." He gulped the soda, grimacing against the flavor, while searching for the sugar and caffeine. Finished, he crushed the can and threw it at Layla who appreciated the attention. "Nobody tells your old man where he's not welcome." He smiled his most radiant, bloody smile at his son, trying to instill in the boy a sense of moral outrage at the idea some mere mortal would dictate a damn thing to a Hickerson.

Wendell knew the look. He'd practiced his own in the mirror at home. He knew exactly what it was meant to convey and, despite misgivings about his father's philosophy and fiber, felt a swell of pride pushing out from on top of his stomach.

"Where's my truck?"

Wendell shrugged.

"You see it when you picked me up?" Wendell shook his head. Shit. Probably Cal had made an escape in it. They had an understanding about scrapes like that. First sign of trouble it was every man for himself. "Your mom know where you are?"

"She might guess."

Terry nodded slowly. "She might at that." He smiled. "You're gonna catch hell, son."

Wendell beamed. "Yep."

"C'mon. Let's get some food, then."

Layla rode between them, which his mom would kill him for later, placing her muddy paws all over the seat and then jumping in back and painting the windows on either side with saliva and snot. Terry cracked the windows and Layla shoved her snout into the crevice, licking the top of the glass and barking enthusiastically every time they stopped.

His father insisted that Wendell drive as he had a headache anyway. "Can't crawl back inside your momma's cold womb and live, boy. You don't drive by now, probably never will." His father lit a cigarette, another thing Wendell would catch hell for, and closed his eyes. "Why don't you find us some tunes?"

Wendell was overwhelmed with excitement and responsibility and nearly dropped them over the side of the mountain, trying to find a good radio station. He pulled the wheel too sharp, overcompensating for their drift, but his father never said a word. Never even glared at him. Wendell found a southern rock station and paused, his fingers hovering over the dial, waiting to hear confirmation or dismissal of his choice. Terry just sank lower into his seat and placed his left foot on the dash. Every few seconds, he would mumble along with the music, his voice rising for the few words he seemed to know and dropping down again immediately after. "...fly like an eagle...into the future..."

Wendell was piloting his father's seemingly improvised directions until they'd passed anything familiar to him. The elder Hickerson bade his son further and further south and east, finally instructing him to circle on back to a convenience mart they'd just passed.

"Slow down, boy. Keep going, keep going."

They idled across the street on the road's gravel shoulder like tourists consulting a map until the lone car in the parking lot drove away.

"Okay. Easy, now, like I told you. Pull up and keep it running. Give the horn a blast if anybody's coming."

Terry pulled a plastic grocery bag out of his back pocket and slipped it over his swelled-up head. He pulled it taut over his face with his left hand and used the index and middle finger of his right to poke himself in the eyes, gouging small holes therein. He produced a pistol from the back of his waistband, checked it was loaded and he was out the door.

MONDALE

He still wasn't back to his usual self by the time the Assistant State's Attorney made it to town. The visit from Eileen and the phone calls with Shirley had wrecked him for a week or so. Figured eventually he'd bounce back. Or crawl anyway. But he was still in a shit mood.

The ASA was a young guy. Political animal. Mondale understood. Chowder Thompson would make a good-looking trophy to mount behind the desk in his office. Was even a time, years ago, Mondale may've even been inclined to help him do it. But he'd grown the hell up.

Chowder Thompson was more than a necessary evil, he

was citizen number-one as far as Jimmy was concerned. The taxes from Darlin's last year, funneled through the bait store, had paid for the day care program at the high school as well as improvements to the courthouse and computers for the sheriff's department. Like what he did and supplied or not, Chowder was good for Spruce.

Between himself and Chowder, they'd got vice regulated and out of the way of those inclined to frown on it. They'd kept regional outfits as well as bike gangs and the new crop of Mexicans pushing north from taking a piece of Hamilton County. But this crusader with the fancy suit and airs of moral rectitude wanted to bring all of it down. Jimmy'd be damned if he'd let that happen.

"Sheriff, thanks for taking the time to see me. Dennis Jordan, pleasure." He extended a clean, smooth hand toward Jimmy, who took it and gave a good show of returning the smile.

"Sure thing."

"Sheriff, I won't keep you long, but I wanted to put a face to your name, as I've been reading it so often. Don't you find that you learn so much more from talking to someone face to face than from reading about them in a deposition?"

"How's that, exactly?"

The young lawyer took his hand back and sat down across from him. "As I explained on the phone, I am looking into Charles Thompson." He didn't wait for Jimmy to acknowledge that he had heard. "As Sheriff of Hamilton County I'm sure you've had occasion to know of Mr. Thompson and his activities."

"I know Chowder, sure. I know he used to ride with the Bucs, I'm sure had some wild times, but far as I know, these days he's just a business man. I've had no problems with him."

Dennis Jordan cocked his head slightly and smiled coyly. "Forgive my bluntness, Sheriff, but I just don't believe that." He straightened in his seat and Jimmy leaned back in his. "I don't believe Chowder Thompson is an upright citizen and I don't believe that you think so either."

Mondale laced his fingers and rested his elbows on the arms of his chair. He put his chin to his knuckles. "Well, I suppose that's your constitutional right."

"It is. Well put, Sheriff. Have you heard any of the old stories about Mr. Thompson's time with the Bucs?"

Mondale shrugged. "Never been too interested in rumors."

"No, of course not. Can't go prosecuting anything based on rumors. But surely they've grabbed your interest now and again?"

"Seems the Bucs ran crank and dope, maybe some weapons. ATF, DEA, FBI never made anything of it. But, like I said, just rumors and Chowder's not been with the Bucs in nearly fifteen years. I haven't heard any rumors about him attending any churches recently, but that's *his* constitutional right."

"Sheriff, can I tell you one of my favorite rumors about Mr. Thompson?" The young lawyer didn't wait for Mondale's consent. "Apparently the Bucs had something of a sensitive spot about federal informants – got really paranoid sometimes – anyway, one time they'd discovered a possible informant among them and they left the Q&A to Mr. Thompson." The lawyer leaned into the story, emphasizing with both hands. "First thing Chowder did was take out his buddy's left eyeball with a spoon. No questions, he just figured that rumor alone was enough to take that much action on. Then he fries it up like an egg at the campfire and eats it with Tabasco sauce." Dennis Jordan smiled and shook his head. "I don't know about you, but that kind of autonomy sure could get me a better record. I bet you could use a little more legal wiggle-room sometimes too, huh?"

Both men were silent a moment, then the attorney continued. "Point I'm making, Sheriff, is that Charles Thompson will never pay anything back, legally speaking, for that little rumor, but it's one of many that I'd like to see him go down for. What I need, and what I'm going to get, is hard evidence to prosecute him on and I'm going to put him and anyone else he's working with away for a long time."

Mondale nodded slowly. "Yeah, that's one I heard too. Never asked him about it though."

The attorney smiled again. "Like you say, they're just rumors. You have to hold on to them loosely. But I've made my mind up about Charles Thompson."

That movie-star grin dropped all warmth as it grew wider. "What I've not yet made up my mind about, Sheriff, is you."

Jimmy stiffened and said, "How do you mean?" with what he hoped sounded like an absence of panic.

"I'm trying to decide if you're just a backwater hick with a badge, sitting on his thumbs oblivious to the criminal enterprise of Chowder Thompson or…" his smile dropped, "…or if you're his partner."

Cocksucker.

TERRY

He'd spent the next few days recuperating. His face looked like ground beef that had maybe been stepped on a little bit. His nose had broken, but he'd had worse, and his missing tooth added an extra wicked dimension to his smile. The swelling pulled his skin tight and the bruising turned shades of purple and high-yellow before settling into a baby-shit brown, but the truth was he looked far worse than he felt. He'd passed out chuckling while that big dyke beat on him, offering nothing but token defense. The earful he'd gotten from Beth after Wendell'd taken her car again was more unpleasant than the whuppin.

He didn't bother checking with the plant, as he was sure his job was forfeit by Wednesday, so Thursday he went looking for Cal again. He was pretty sure his pal had the keys to his truck and for that oversight would buy at least the first round.

Before his walk, he showered, shaved and put on fresh jeans and tucked a neatly rolled t-shirt into his back pocket. When he got to town, he put the shirt on and stepped into the drug store. He nodded to Sylvi at the cash register and proceeded to the newsstand. He grabbed a girly rag then made his way to the phone. He dropped a quarter in the slot. He knew the number by heart.

"Yeah?"

"Cal Dotson there?"

"Hold on." From the far end, he heard the clunk of a receiver hitting the counter and a far away voice call, "Dotson. Phone call." Another voice said "Who is it?" and was answered, "Don't be giving out this number, asshole. Gonna cut you off."

He heard the fumbling sound of the receiver lifted and then, "Yeah?"

"It's me."

"Terry?"

"You got the keys to my chariot?"

"Oh, shit."

"Yeah no shit, oh shit. Come get me."

"Where are you?"

"Blaylock Drug."

"Why aren't you at work?" Terry didn't answer. He let him think about it a minute. "Oh, shit. Yeah, yeah I'll be right over."

He hung up and leaned back against the wall, opening *Swank*. Terry thumbed over to the letters section and rolled his eyes while he read one about a guy who caught the neighbor ballin his old lady, so he goes over and fucks the neighbor's wife and then the four of them started getting together for group gropes. He wondered if it was a true story. Probably not.

Every time he picked up a smut piece, first thing, he scoured it for signs of Ponch's work. Ponch always signed different names, but used certain phrases and words in all of his work as a sort of signature. He found nothing resembling the Mexican scribe in *Swank*.

He felt the disapproving eyes of Sylvi on him from across the store and looked up. She was pretending to do busy work, stocking gum and dusting fixtures, but she shot him glances every few seconds to let him know he was being watched.

From the front of the store came the bell sound announcing someone entering. Sylvi spoke up, for Terry's benefit, no doubt. "Mornin, Sheriff."

Terry smiled, putting his tongue into the previously toothy void and licking his lips. He looked up and saw the sheriff pacing through the store, coming straight toward him, far as he could tell. Here he comes, thought Terry, King Fucker can't quite smell the princess on me, but he knows something is different.

Mondale gave Terry a slow nod, "You look like you saw your wife recently."

Terry's smile was harmless, but his eyes were radioactive.

The sheriff passed him by, on his way to the refrigerated drinks, "You give Beth my best, if you see her."

"Sure, thing, Sheriff. Likewise," he added with a salacious wink at the sheriff's back.

Mondale seemed tense, but he turned around and nodded with cautious geniality at Terry. "How is your family, Hickeson?"

"Oh real good, Sheriff, thanks for asking. My boy, he's about that age now, sticks his pecker in any keyhole he can find. I try and teach him safe sex, though. Be careful of splinters, I always say." He dropped his smile as indication of the seriousness of the subject he was about to broach. "Now, Sheriff, I ain't pointing fingers, but if you have any complaints about molested animals, pets and such around town, you let me know. I'll look real close at the boy. You know how they go there for a few years."

His smile returned and he added, "How's your family? Thought I saw your little one round here a while back."

There was a tap of the horn from Cal's truck outside. Terry waved him in from the front window. Cal left the car running and came in the front door, making the bells jingle. He skipped a beat when he saw the sheriff, but nodded gentleman-like at Sylvi and said, "Ma'am."

"Give me five dollars," said Terry. Cal didn't ask why, just handed over the dampest, limpest Lincoln Terry'd ever handled.

He paid for the magazine and on his way out the door he called to Mondale, "If you see her, tell her that I thought she looked good, Sheriff. Real good." He winked. "I bet they make you proud."

Some days were just beautiful.

Terry's freedom from the oppressive bonds of employment had given the world a rosy hue. After he filed for unemployment, Cal drove them back to The Gulch to get their shit straight.

"I'm telling you bro, Branson's full of rich faggots." Cal did most of his best thinking after a couple of pitchers. "I'm telling you we need to find us one and squeeze him."

Terry took the high road for once and didn't touch that one. "How do you suggest we do that?"

"We just find one that's well to do and got sense enough not to want his habits known and then threaten if he don't give us a bunch of money that we'll tell everybody he's limber of butthole."

"Uh-huh." Terry turned it over for a few minutes then said, "And why would anybody believe us?"

"We'll have pictures."

Terry did not like this development. "Count me out. I may be pretty, but I ain't going to seduce any pervert no matter how much money he's got." He killed his mug and poured some more. "And I sure as hell don't feature taking any pictures of your hairy nuts on some dude's chin." Terry shuddered at the image he'd just given himself.

Cal choked on his Bud, a thin trickle escaped his nostril and lost itself in the stubble of his upper lip. "Don't even say it, man. It ain't even like that." Cal wiped his mouth and nose on the shoulder of his shirt, as the sleeves had been trimmed away long ago when Cal's upper arms had a bit more in the way of defining features. "Nah, there's this place, this bar where they all get together and pretend it's normal. I seen it once."

"I believe it."

"Listen to me, all we gotta do is get some good pictures of somebody inside."

"What'll that prove?"

"What country do you live in? It'll look plenty queer and that's all we'll need."

Terry leaned back in his seat. He felt himself slipping into deep thought so he took another shot to nip that in the bud. "Huh."

CHOWDER

Hettie'd gone to fat years ago, but she still had it. When she turned over, the sheet slipped off her hip. Chowder looked at the serpent inked into her side, faded now and stretched some, it coiled round betwixt her bosoms and under the right one then down her ribs, hooking on the hip, tracing the hitch of her ass cheek, passing between her legs and up so that her inner thigh featured the head, fangs bared and ready to take your dick off. He reached out and smacked her ass hard. The cellulite jiggle might've lasted forever, but she sprang up out of slumber and coldcocked him instinctively.

"Ow, fucker."

Chowder frowned and rubbed his jaw. "Who you calling fucker, cow?"

"Pencil dick."

"Bitch." He pulled the sheet down exposing his own inked torso and grabbed his penis. He squeezed it and wagged it at her. Hettie punched him in the stomach, then got on her knees on the bed and bent over, taking him in her mouth. Chowder let go of himself and ran his hands through her hair, kneading the back of her neck and shoulders while she worked on him.

While he watched her head bob, he straightened himself and she responded by digging her head further beneath his gut. As her head disappeared from view, he focused on that big ol' ass of hers waving higher in the air. He clamped onto it with both hands, pushing her gently, but firmly, down. His grip tightened, then he slapped it and she grunted in response. He felt just a hint of teeth at the base of his pecker and it sent a shiver through him that ended with Hettie getting up and retreating to the bathroom to spit and gargle.

He lay back and briefly enjoyed his cleared head. Leisurely, he skimmed the edges of his consciousness for something worth fixing on. He thought about Hettie back when they'd met. That snake tattoo had just about been the sexiest thing he'd ever seen and it held a power over him from the first time he saw it. When she'd told him she was pregnant by him he'd married her the next day and when Irm had come along, it'd seemed like the most natural progression of events to quit the Bucs and make a home somewhere.

The plan hadn't come all at once and they'd been in no rush to conceive one. Hettie told him that he was in charge and she'd go along with whatever he said. The underlying, but unspoken understanding was as long as you say the right thing. That's the way it'd always been between them. Even when she was mad at him, and he'd given her reason to be a time or two, she never said anything but how he was in charge. He was the man. His was the responsibility to lead and hers was to follow. But damn, when she said it, it didn't have the effect of making him free. Rather she'd bound him to her more tightly. She never busted his balls about other women long as he didn't rub her nose in it and when he did eventually leave the Bucs, ten years later, and took her and Irm to the Missouri hills without a word of what he had in mind, she never complained.

She was a hell of a woman and he was a lucky man.

He was more than lucky, though. He was good. He ran a good business. Chowder's Bait 'N More was a money-maker on its own, but Darlin's had made it a cornerstone of the local economy. Now some shitweasel was trying to bring him down and he needed to put a name and face on that threat quick. Until he knew for sure, it remained between him and the sheriff, the only two he could be a hundred percent sure of.

He couldn't even tell his wife or daughter. Not that he believed Irm or Hettie would ever turn on him, but he couldn't be sure how they'd handle the knowledge that somebody was talking to the government.

There was a sound from the bathroom that he registered as the top popping off of a pill bottle and then the running faucet. The door opened and Hettie stood there, hair pulled back in a tail, breasts supported by her round gut looking angry, hungry and mean. She held a green plastic cup of tap water in one hand and a little blue pill in the other.

Chowder rolled over and pulled the sheet over his head. Hettie's voice was full of authority. "Oh hell no. You don't get off that easy."

CHAPTER EIGHT

MONDALE

The stretch of 71b that led south from Neosho toward the Arkansas border was a gold mine for speeding tickets. The two lane highway wound through the hills with speed limits jumping from sixty-five to forty-five, then up to fifty-five every few minutes with a traffic signal or two thrown in to further complicate things. A cruiser placed around any bend or in the parking lot of a convenience mart was a sure fire money-maker for all of the hamlets dotting the map, including Spruce.

Mondale sat in his own prowler along the path to Pineville for hours. The sun had set on him and he'd not issued a single ticket. He'd sat in silence and now in darkness going over the situation with the ASA endlessly.

Mondale'd just about punched the little shit when he'd expressed open suspicion of him. But he hadn't, and wondered now if he should've. What he'd done instead was call him an arrogant little prick and ask him to leave.

As soon as the lawyer had left the building, Jimmy told

Wanda he was leaving and had blown off Bob Musil who approached him in the parking lot with a flat upraised hand. Deputy Musil swallowed whatever he had to say and let Jimmy go. He'd not answered any radio calls the rest of the day, finally switching the damn thing off when he parked.

Some things had become clear in the meantime. Dennis Jordan didn't have anything on him. He'd never tip his hand like that if he was sitting on good information, he'd just have him arrested at the right time. It was also clear to Mondale that he had to take another look at his partner. Their fates were tied so closely that he couldn't afford to be lax in any part of their operation. Chowder was a damn good businessman and had muscle enough that Jimmy'd been able to steer clear of his side of the business and let the big man run it how he saw fit, but something was wrong and Jimmy couldn't feature it being on his end. Outside of Deputy Musil, whom he trusted implicitly, there wasn't anybody with any idea what he was up to.

Lights appeared around the bend followed quickly by a familiar pickup truck. Jimmy recognized Tate Dill through the window and Tate nodded at him as he passed. He watched the truck disappear around the next bend. His fingers flexed instinctively and he blinked. Jimmy started the car.

Tate pulled over after a couple of miles when he noticed he was being followed. Mondale hadn't hit his lights or siren and Tate didn't look nervous sitting there, but Jimmy's hairs had been standing since the truck had passed him. He left his headlights on and exited the vehicle.

The dark was complete now and nothing could be seen outside the cast of the prowler's beams. They were pulled over to the gravel shoulder of the narrow highway with an incline to their left and a sharp bank on the road's right side. The tall trees could be heard waving in the breeze, but not seen towering over them. The crunch of his boots as he stepped sounded sharply over the low purring of the vehicles' motors.

He could see Tate's elbow hanging out the open window and resting on the door. Inside the truck, Jimmy saw him adjust the rearview mirror. The prickly sensation on his skin moved, but didn't go away and Jimmy fought his instincts to have a hand on his hip by his gun. He wanted to keep this casual.

Tate's left arm moved as he drew parallel to the window and he saw Tate take a drag from the joint he held. Tate nodded at the policeman while he held his breath. As he exhaled he said, "Hey, Sheriff, how you doing tonight?"

"Evening, Tate. What's going on?"

Tate, still exhaling with his lips, turned in and shook his head gently. "Nothin. Beautiful night though, huh?" Mondale looked into his unfocused, red-rimmed eyes, but saw no sign of nerves.

"The hell are you doing?"

Tate looked ready to repeat what he'd just said. Jimmy pointed at the joint. "I mean with that."

"Oh, sorry." Tate offered it to the Sheriff.

"Turn off the engine and get out the truck, Tate." Tate blinked and did a double take. "Now."

"What's up, Jimmy?" He turned off his engine and opened the door and Mondale backed up to give him room to step out.

"Turn around and put your hands on the hood."

"Sure, Jimmy." He was confused, but still didn't sound concerned. "What should I do with this?" He indicated the joint.

"Drop it."

"Okay."

Mondale took his flashlight out and ran it over the interior of the pickup while Tate leaned on the hood, staring at the fading cherry on the joint's tip between his feet in the gravel. Finding nothing worth looking at, he returned his attention to Tate. "Turn around."

"What's going on, Jimmy?"

"I'm the damn police, Tate, not your friend." This registered only an uncomprehending stare from Tate Dill. "So pot's still illegal, shithead."

Tate slumped. "Oh, man. C'mon, Jimmy, you weren't flashing lights, I just figured it was a social stop."

"Hey," he slapped the back of Tate's head. "We don't have a social relationship. What are you doing out here tonight?"

Tate shrugged innocently. "Just driving, Jimmy. Going to work."

"Uh-huh. Well, now you're going to jail."

"What? Why are you being such a prick, Jimmy? C'mon, I gotta go to work. Chowder's gonna kill me if I'm late." Jimmy looked at him hard. His eyes were more confused and scared than angry. Mondale's hair began to lie down again. "C'mon, Jimmy, please. If I did something that pissed you off, I'm sorry, man, but I don't know about it, really."

"Shit." Mondale relaxed and gestured at the joint on the ground. "Pick that up." Tate did. It had gone out and he held it sideways, pinched between his fingers uncertainly. Mondale raised his eyebrows and Tate cocked his head.

"What?"

"It don't work unless you burn it." Tate got his lighter out of his pocket and placed the joint in his lips. He got it lit and offered it to the sheriff. Mondale accepted it and took a quick hit. He held it at his side then and after another moment, took a deeper hit before handing it back to Tate. "Take it easy."

Tate took the joint and watched Mondale walk back to his vehicle. "You alright, Sheriff?"

TERRY

The inside of Terry's truck smelled like someone had pelted it with a bottle of cologne. Between the two of them, they'd spritzed on more vapor-aids and hair treatment in one night than the rest of their lives combined. Terry insisted that they crack the windows as their hygiene fumes were threatening to overwhelm him and succeeding on at least making his head hurt.

Cal's wisps of red hair were clumped together with gel and Terry could see freckles abounding across his shiny white scalp. His own head-top hair, too long by six weeks, was curling at the ends and separating from the upward tending mass on the back of his neck. Terry tugged at the base of his skull constantly while he drove.

"You look fine," said Cal and smiled at his friend when Terry turned to glare at him.

"You saying I look like a queer?"

"No."

"Well that's too bad. Cause that's exactly the look we're going for, right?"

There was a moment's pause then Cal quietly said, "No."

"No?"

"I'm trying to look good *to* a queer, not look *like* a queer."

Terry sneered and shook his head sadly. "Afraid I've got bad news on both fronts."

The bar was a non-descript, aluminum-sided ranch-style with a gravel parking lot out front and an abandoned gas station across the road, twenty miles outside of Branson. It looked like one of the hard-rode titty bars with wood-plank walks and railings seen in old cowboy movies, that you'd find tucked away just off the interstate every ten miles or so, except for the lack of lighted signage to draw anybody's eye. Not even a neon Budweiser to call attention to it. If not for the two vehicles out front, and the half-dozen more around the back, it looked closed.

They parked at one of the dry pumps across the two-lane and studied it. "You sure that's it?" asked Terry.

Cal nodded. "I know. You'd expect it to look fruitier outside, but that's the place."

After ten minutes of pre-game 40s in the truck, they approached the building. Indoors it wasn't any fruitier. It was dark and cleanish, but still a saloon. Juke in one corner next to a Mortal Kombat machine, video-poker on the bar and a couple pool tables in the back. They took seats at the bar and ordered more beers, then looked around at the other clientele. "I dunno if this is gonna work," said Terry. "A photo of this place'll look like a picture of any other bar. We need something really really like super-gay if we're gonna blackmail anybody with it."

Cal nodded then pointed out. "Notice there aren't any women around, though." Cal re-checked, then continued. "Speaks loud and clear." He raised his eyebrows in support of this point.

Terry counted the entire female population of the place up to zero, then asked, "How many women you ever seen back home at The Gulch?"

Cal dismissed the thought. "That's different."

Shaking his head, Terry said, "Not in a photograph, it's not. C'mon, let's go."

"No way, I'ma finish my beer and have another." Cal's pride was hurt. "Since this place is so much like our place, I don't see why not."

"Don't get pouty. It was a good plan, but let's stick to liquor stores and bait shops for now." The bartender eyed them warily and Terry signaled for another pitcher. "'Sides, who am I kidding? Like we're really gonna drive all the way out here and not see Yakoff? I don't think so."

After the second pitcher, Cal needed to take a leak. "Come with me."

"Why?"

"Think I'm gonna let myself get cruised in a queer piss shack? Uh-uh, I need back up." They found the restroom and Cal put his ear to the door before opening it. Hearing nothing untoward, he went through, but asked Terry to stay back and stand sentry. "Changed my mind. It'd look bad, both of us going in together." Terry nodded and slumped against the wall.

He'd never been to a gay bar before. Heard of them, but never been. Not that he'd spent much time thinking about it, but this really wasn't what he'd imagined. Buncha blue collar types mostly, letting their wrists dangle a bit, but otherwise pretty conservative. There were a couple of grease monkeys just coming in, headed for the corner to shoot pool. There was a businessman, fat and bald, but dressed sharp and letting his money talk to the young blonde on the far side of the bar. Dynamics seemed familiar. Still, he figured if he were a queer he'd probably just stay at home and jerk off looking at himself in the mirror.

When he returned from the bathroom Cal was more than a little befuddled to see Terry talking up the mechanics shooting pool on the far side of the room. Terry seemed not at all put at odds with his surroundings which Cal found unsettling, but his curiosity won out and he put on his easiest smile as he approached.

Terry and the one mechanic were talking about trucks and transmissions, one and then the other pantomiming shifting from reverse to first and on up. Unless it was code of some sort. Homo-jackoff sign language. That would be like Terry to learn the vulgar bits first. Only.

"Hoah, Terry, you ready to go?"

"Nah, c'mon, let's stay awhile, this here faggot is my cousin Stuart. We knocked over one of my first grocery stores together with his dad's squirrel gun." Stuart mimed aiming the gun awkwardly at Terry who opened a mock cash register and began pulling out bills.

Cal looked uneasy.

"Don't worry, they know we're not into sex with each other. It's cool."

Terry and Stuart shot pool for a half-hour, and, after failing to find conversational common ground with Cal, the other mechanic relocated to the bar, leaving Cal sitting alone on a stool along the wall, when Terry's laugh rang out loud and familiar. He was responding to something Stuart had said.

"The fuck out."

Stuart's fingers made the Scout's Honor sign. "Swear."

"No. "

"Yeah."

"How many of our cousins did you blow?"

"I ain't telling you."

"Why not?"

"'Cause it's maybe a private thing, or don't you know anything about those?" Terry, well into his drinks, doubled over giggling and Stuart looked as if he were enjoying the reunion as much as his cousin was. "Hey, played your cards right, could've happened for you too."

Terry choked on his drink and spit it on the floor. "How about now?" he barely managed.

Stuart stood straighter. "No chance, cousin. I've got standards."

"Hey, Cal, take a picture of me and Stu." Terry put his arm around his cousin and they straightened up and grinned for Cal who framed them quickly in the camera he'd brought for extortion purposes. The flash brought some nervous glances their way, but they were ignored.

The three of them shot pool for another half hour. Cal listened to stories about their family and childhood, early heists and updates on various folks fallen by the way. When he returned with a fresh pitcher, Terry's eyes glinted and his posture was conspiratorial. He suggested they find a seat and Stuart led the way to a table where they sat and drew the circle tight.

Terry looked at his cousin and told him why they were there.

"So, who should we pay attention to here?"

Stuart looked back and forth between them. "Are you serious?" Terry nodded solemnly. "You want me to suggest someone for you to blackmail?"

Terry looked at Cal, then back to Stuart. "Look, we don't know anybody here besides you and we're not gonna do nothing to you or one of your friends, but if you could help us out, we'd appreciate it."

Stuart sat up straight. "Fuck you, Terry. I'm not going to do that. What do you think I am?" Terry and Cal exchanged puzzled glances then Cal spoke up.

"If you give us a good lead, we could cut you in. Y'know, sort of like a finder's fee."

Terry nodded. "Consultant's fee, damn straight. What do you say, cousin?" Stuart looked back and forth between them for a sign that this was a joke, but Terry continued. "Like I said, we don't wanna mess with you, but" he leaned in closer "maybe there's somebody you'd like to mess with? Somebody deserves it?"

Anger flared briefly behind Stuart's eyes, but it was eventually replaced by wonder and then resign. "Okay."

"Alright." Cal rubbed his hands together.

Stuart held up a hand, "But I don't want any money. I'm not doing this for any reason other than he's a real dick and you're my cousin."

Cal nodded. "Sure, then. Who is it?"

Terry licked his lip and arched his eyebrows.

Stuart rolled his eyes and nodded with his gaze across the room. "See the dude in the wig chatting up my friend Russell?"

With utter nonchalance, Terry and Cal looked over their shoulders and saw the back of the man's head. From their angle they couldn't tell much about him other than he was slight and probably in his late forties. It was definitely a wig he wore, a near shoulder length blonde-bob, which clashed with his conservative clothes; light blue jeans with a brown leather belt and a vertically striped button down tucked into them. He wore grey colored tennis shoes with white socks and leaned against the bar with his head balanced on his left fist looking intently, it seemed, at Russell, engrossed in whatever he was saying.

Terry and Cal turned back to Stuart who said, "You know who that is?" They looked at each other and shrugged.

"Who is he?"

Stuart stood up to leave. "He's the one you want, but don't do anything tonight, 'cause everybody'll remember you were here with me."

"Who is that, Stu?"

Stuart shook his head. "Go home and watch some TV, channel fifty-one, then come back next week. He comes by all the time, puts on that stupid wig and a ridiculous accent, thinks nobody recognizes him." Stuart glared at the man's back then turned to Terry. "Asshole deserves it, just leave me out. Good to see you, cousin." Stuart walked out of the bar.

Cal and Terry turned around and tried to get a better look at the man throwing a wrist and giggling at something hee-larry-us Russell had to say. Cal said, "Your cousin's pretty cool. What's on channel fifty-one? You think he's like a weather guy or something?"

Terry shook his head. "Nah, man, fifty-one is the religious station."

CHAPTER NINE

CHOWDER

Tate Dill was leaning on the counter flipping through a glossy magazine when Chowder opened the front door. The doofus looked up at him and nodded then went back to his reading. "Where's Irm?" Chowder asked. Irm hadn't spoken to him for two weeks. He couldn't decide if he was glad about that or not. The swelling at her eye had gone down, but the bruising of her pride would take longer to heal.

Tate shook his head slowly without looking up from his magazine. "Dunno. Thought maybe you was her coming in for her shift."

Chowder went behind the counter and into the back office. "She hasn't shown up yet?"

"No. Haven't seen her since yesterday. She's still not talking."

Chowder grabbed the telephone and dialed his daughter's number. When the voice mail picked up he left a gruff message. "Get your ass in to work." He wheeled the rolling chair over to the safe and spun the dial with his thumb. "How long you been here, Tate?"

"Since this morning." He appeared in the doorway a moment later. "I don't mind staying, but if you could hold down the fort while I go grab a bite, I'd appreciate it."

Chowder counted through the deposit from the day before and double-checked the reports. Without looking up he said, "Give me five minutes, then you can take off."

"Sure?"

"Yeah, just lemme get a couple things in order."

"Okay." Tate went back to the counter. The receipts from Darlin's had been down since the incident with Irm a couple weeks back, and Chowder suspected that had to do with Irm's nastier than usual demeanor. Now she wasn't even picking up her shifts at the bait shop? At least Tate was stepping up. He didn't ever complain or offer an opinion on anything. Chowder liked that. He hated the thought of going outside his family for important work, but Irm wasn't leaving him much choice these days.

He glanced at the security camera feed. Tate was alone, stocking a few items before leaving. Chowder watched the kid work and thought about the future. Truth was, he was getting a little itchy for the horizon these days. The headaches were starting to pile up and Mondale's announcement about a new investigation and the possibility of an informant? He'd like to disappear with Hettie for the rest of his life. Just the two of them with a pocketful of cash. Gulf of Mexico maybe. That'd be okay.

Hettie came in an hour later. He'd called her and asked if Irm had checked in.

"No. Why?"

"She's blowing off work. Come on up to the shop and bring dinner, huh?"

And now she'd arrived. Hettie came through the front door and held up two plastic bags full of food.

The round woman turned sideways to pass behind the counter. She kissed Chowder's cheek. "Surprised you didn't just eat some junk food. Lord knows you sell enough of it here."

"Nah, I knew you'd come through." She'd brought cold chicken and gravy for sandwiches, potato salad and asparagus sticks. He got off his stool and shuffled over to the aisle with plastic ware, selected some and tore it open on the way back to the office. Hettie was putting out the spread. He set the plates and utensils down and went out for another chair. When he came back into the office, they sat across from each other and Hettie handed out the sandwiches.

She kicked her feet up and burrowed them snugly into Chowder's crotch. Chowder licked a drop of cold gravy off his fingers and spoke with a mouthful. "Feel like taking a trip?"

Hettie grabbed a napkin and, leaning forward, wiped a drop of gravy off of his pants. "Where to?"

"Someplace warm, I'm thinking."

"Sounds nice. When?"

Chowder went to the refrigerator and returned with a chocolate milk for himself and Diet Coke for his wife. "Soon as I can afford it." She accepted the pop and opened it. She slurped the fizzy top bit before it could spill and Chowder continued. "Just something I've been thinking about recently. Getting out. For good."

"Really? That's new."

"Maybe, but I think it's the best idea I've had in a long time."

"You're the idea man."

"How would you like it? To leave? Retire."

"I'd give it a try."

The front door bells rang and Chowder looked at the security video feed as two big, camo-decked fishermen headed straight for the cooler.

"Well give it some serious thought, but don't say nothing to anybody."

Hettie picked up and asparagus stick and paused with it between her front teeth. "What about Irm?"

Chowder wiped his mouth with his sleeve and got up to see to the customers making their way to the front counter on the video feed. "'Specially not her."

When Irm came through the front, two hours later, she went to the office and shut the door. Chowder's stomach cramped and he belched. Tasted asparagus. He sold some night crawlers and a case of Tab to the citizen at the counter. He looked at the time then and held his breath waiting for his daughter to come out.

Irm emerged from the office two minutes later and went immediately to the coffee pot and poured herself a helping before pulling up a stool to sit on behind the counter. Chowder turned, leaning on the counter, to look at her full-on. The swelling had disappeared, but there was still a trace of purple gone to yellow receding like the tide in a half moon around her right eye. She didn't look at him or say anything, instead picked up his magazine and began to flip through it.

"You're fuckin fired, you know that, right?"

"Sure."

"Where were you tonight?"

"Nowhere." She flipped a page of the magazine and leaned in to study a photo of a celebrity's cellulite. "Here, if anybody asks."

"Who'd ask?"

"Nobody." She tilted the magazine as if to get a better angle of the movie star's thighs. "Sheriff, maybe."

"The hell you been doing, Irma? Tell me."

She looked up at her father with calm defiance. "Nothing."

"Well you're fucking fired."

"You said that."

"Yeah well, don't miss any more shifts."

MONDALE

A twenty-four box of corn dogs in the frozen foods section caught his eye and he picked it up guiltily. Seemed he'd read somewhere that you should never do the grocery shopping when you were hungry. Maybe there was something to that, but he was hungry and stressed and knew that these batter dipped shit sticks were going to hit the spot.

He stood in the line thinking about the best way to prepare them. If he weren't so hungry, he'd heat the oven and get them nice and crispy on the outside, but there was no way he'd have the patience for that. His skill with a microwave was non-existent. He'd simultaneously burn and undercook them if he tried that, so he was left with pan-frying them, which still required vigilance. Low heat, he kept telling himself. Give em a chance to warm through before scorching the outside. Use some butter, not oil, to keep em from sticking.

"Hey, Jimmy." He snapped out of concentration and turned his head to see who'd spoken his name. "Looks like it's going to be a good night." Behind him Eileen's friend Julie Sykes was indicating his box of corn dogs and twelve pack of High Life with a coy smile he tried hard to not find sexy.

"Hey, Julie, yeah these are pretty good. Winning combination." Despite himself, his cheeks colored some.

"Been a long time since I've had a corn dog."

It was harder than he thought it should be not to find a suggestion in there. He examined her basket full of various vegetables and greens. "Hah. I guess so." He turned to face front again, but couldn't stay so. Over his shoulder he said, "Thanks for letting Eileen stay with you."

"Oh, no problem. I always liked Eileen."

"She knows she could stay with me if she wanted to, but well, I'm sure she'd rather stay with her friends. Think I'd probably cramp her style."

Behind him Julie snorted. "Me too, Jimmy."

"How's that?"

"Oh, Eileen's got her own style. Always had."

"Yeah, I suppose you're right." He set the box of corn dogs and the beer on the conveyer belt and smiled at the cashier. What's her name? Glenda. "How're you tonight, Glenda?"

Glenda the cashier smiled. "Fine, Sheriff, you?"

"Fine. Fine." The transaction completed and Mondale refused a sack to put his dinner in. Glenda began to ring up Julie's groceries as the thought occurred to him, he'd like a pack of cigarettes. "Oh, could I get a pack of Marlboros?" He'd said it before noticing it was too late.

Glenda indicated the line behind them and said, "Sorry, Sheriff. You'll have to get back in line."

Julie said, "Go ahead and ring em up on my ticket." She smiled at Jimmy, who looked embarrassed.

Glenda finished the transaction and Julie handed over the pack of smokes. They walked out of the grocery store together and Jimmy stopped outside the door to fiddle with the wrapping on the Marlboros. "Hold on Julie, I've got cash for you." He fumbled with the plastic wrapping and tore it open gracelessly. He dropped the cellophane into the trash and found a lighter in his pocket. He sparked it and began digging for cash, but Julie stopped him.

"That's okay. How bout you cook me dinner?"

Mondale raised the box of corn dogs to eye level. "Spose I could spare one or two."

What the hell was he doing?

He preheated the oven, opting for sure-fire deliciousness, since he was entertaining. He cracked a High Life for himself and one for Julie, who'd made space on his kitchen counter to make a large salad. He didn't allow himself to think about anything he was doing and, had he allowed a reflective thought to surface, would have been disconcerted to find that it was so easy. When the oven was warmed, he loaded a dozen corn dogs onto a cookie sheet and opened two more beers.

By the time they were ready to eat, he'd relaxed considerably. He didn't have anything other than ketchup for dressing, so they ate her salad dry, but he didn't mind. In fact it seemed like the best salad he'd ever had. He'd taken the plastic wrap off a few CDs he'd purchased in the years since Shirley and the girls had left and put something tasteful and unassuming on.

"Sorry 'bout everything, but I haven't entertained in a long time."

"That's alright. I like your place. Feels lived in."

"Has been." He'd moved out for a few months when he and Shirley'd split. She'd gotten the house in the settlement, but he'd bought it back from her when she'd moved away. She'd taken most of the furniture and fixtures that'd been there when they'd built their family, but she'd left him the bed, television and his favorite chair. In the mean time, he'd added a table, a washer and dryer, and a coffee maker.

After dinner, Julie helped him wash dishes in the sink and they'd killed another couple beers. Then, like it was nothing out of the ordinary, she'd got up on the tips of her toes, nipped his lips, and taken her leave. He followed her out onto the porch, the corner of his mouth where she'd kissed him twitching, and he bit his lower lip lest it flare into a smile.

She opened her car door and got behind the wheel, calling out, "Good to see you, Jimmy. Call me if you like, sometime," before starting the car and driving away.

Jimmy went back inside and had two more corn dogs.

He'd spent the week watching channel fifty-one around the clock. It'd started off as research, trying to picture everyone on there in a blonde wig, but his careful scrutiny had given way to fascination with the culture.

One thing he'd decided was that there was a direct relation between the touch of the Holy Spirit and the gift of supernatural hair. He couldn't shake the boldness of their pleas for cash money. How much money did it take to run a television station? *he wondered. He guessed that he could scare up enough scratch to get a license and a camera. There were plenty of folks out there desperate to get on the airwaves he could rent time to. Put up some religious programming – Leave it to Jesus or something – a talk show maybe – live prayer meetings. Take a flat fee or a cut of the donations. That license would pay for itself.*

God, it seemed, was awfully concerned and dismayed at the way people dressed these days and the drugs they enjoyed and the movies they watched. God had a plan to put a stop to it apparently by putting these slick assholes on the airwaves as an example of what an alternative to hedonistic living might look like. For a celestial being in charge of heaven, hell and the cosmos, his preoccupations seemed a tad pedestrian, Terry thought. The ploy would pay off when people on the down slope of a high would flip on the television and become struck with a hunger

for righteousness and straight teeth as modeled by the likes of this one - Brother Eli, the spiritual voice out of Branson.
Brother Eli. Terry thought about him with a blonde wig on.

CHAPTER TEN

TERRY

He and Cal didn't bother to make themselves pretty anymore. They played pool in the corner, quietly surveying the place three nights in a row before they'd caught a glimpse of the bewigged evangelist swishing around the bar. Stuart hadn't been in again. They'd been ignored by the rest of the clientele, and weren't sure how they'd go about getting what they needed.

They huddled at their table and exchanged ideas in excited, hushed tones. "We don't want to draw attention to ourselves," said Cal.

"Too late, kemosabe. We stick out here."

"But we can't just run up and snap pictures off in his face, we're likely to get our butts kicked." He indicated the room full of burly queers. "Even your cousin looked ready to throw a punch when you told him what we was up to."

Terry thought about it. Cal was right. Homos or not, they were seriously outnumbered tonight. The odds weren't in their favor. "So what then? Wait for him to go to the bathroom?"

They thought on that for a few moments. Cal offered, "We need to get him out of here and isolated."

"I told you I'm not doing anything gay."

Cal slapped the table-top. "This is our chance at some real money."

"Hey, we've been over it. You're the one said all we needed was a photo in this place and it would speak for itself."

"I know, but I didn't think it'd be somebody this important. We can totally retire on this one if we do it right, but it can't just be any ol' silly picture in a wig. We need something really, really gay here."

"So you do it. I'll take the picture."

"It's my camera. My idea. I take the picture."

Terry fumed. "Well, I guess we just watch him. Maybe we'll get lucky."

The pace of the night was maddening. Brother Eli floated around the bar getting mostly cold shoulders from the patrons, but it didn't seem to dampen his spirits any.

No new ideas occurred to them. Terry and Cal watched the evangelist with the eyes of lazy predators, stumbled onto the juiciest prey ever. The rate at which nothing was happening troubled them as they felt the breeze drift through their temporal window of opportunity.

Terry felt the weight of destiny on his shoulders as he strode toward the bar for another pitcher. Eli turned to look his direction and Terry averted his eyes and put a slight roll into his hips without thinking about it. He couldn't afford to think about it. This was his big chance. He leaned on the bar awaiting the pitcher and looked steadfastly at the opposite wall while cocking his posture, what he thought might be seductively, toward his mark. The arch in the bartender's eyebrow was subtle, but Terry noticed it and shot him his best *shut the fuck up* look while collecting his order and strutting back to his booth.

When Terry got back, Cal's eyes were as wide as his gaping maw. Terry set the pitcher down. Neither dared to look up or speak above a whisper. The excitement radiating off of his partner had raised the temperature five degrees. Cal's limbs and fingers were positively vibrating with energy.

"That was amazing, dude."

"Shut up." Terry felt queasy.

"You are the man, man."

"I said 'shut the fuck up.'" He clenched his fists to keep from vomiting right there. He was caught somewhere between elation and repulsion, a performance-high and terminal embarrassment.

Cal was having no such conflict. "We are going to be rich, thank you, thank you thank –"

"Hello. What's going on over here in the corner?"

Cal cut his thanks short and Terry looked up into the face of money and knew then what he had to do. Brother Eli in his dorky wig loomed over their table like some fourth grade provocateur in the lunchroom.

He spoke in an exaggerated drawl, "Can I sit down?"

He did so, without invitation, sliding into the booth beside Terry.

"Y'all sure are secretive over here."

Terry didn't trust his own voice enough to speak so he just pounded his beer and put his hand on Eli's thigh. The television preacher reached down for it and gave the hand a squeeze. Then without a word he got up and walked toward the back of the bar and disappeared into the bathroom.

Frantically, Cal fumbled for his camera and spilled his drink in the process.

"Shit shit shit."

He didn't bother cleaning it up. Terry started to drain the pitcher of beer. He'd gotten halfway through it in a minute when Cal said, "Better hurry up, he's likely to change his mind. Here." He extended the camera to Terry.

"I thought you were gonna take the pictures."

"Changed my mind. You do it."

Terry snatched it out of his partner's hand. "Fine. Get the truck ready. Keep it running." Cal nodded and got up, making his way toward the front door. Terry checked the camera and made sure it was ready to go.

Looked like a simple point and click model. The flash was on.

He just about knocked over the table when he stood up. His limbs were awkward and he was jumpy with adrenaline. The walk to the bathroom looked like an impossible distance and he thought he could feel the eyes of the whole world on him as he approached. To steady and steel himself he chanted a mantra under his breath.

Money. Money. Money. Money. Money.

He pushed open the bathroom door. It was dim inside and he didn't see any sign of the preacher. He looked into the mirrored wall above the line of sinks opposite the door and closed it behind him. On the other side of the partition he saw a bank of three urinals and three toilet stalls beyond them. Noiselessly, he crouched down to look for feet. He spied the preacher's tennis shoes planted beneath the first stall. They were all alone. Terry fumbled with the camera that had seemed so small at the table and now felt huge and unwieldy. He tucked it as discreetly as possible underneath his right arm and tested the position for motion. It was no good, so he tucked it into the waist-band of his jeans, against the small of his back, and draped the tail of his shirt over it.

Keeping his instincts in check, Terry walked toward the occupied stall and stopped just outside the door. A groan that teetered on the edge of a purr said, "Come in here." He fixed his grip on Cal's camera with his right hand behind his back.

The door opened slowly and revealed the minister sitting splay-legged on the toilet with his jeans down around his ankles. Brother Eli's cock was up and gripped firmly at the base by his right hand while his left steadied him by clutching the top of the toilet paper dispenser. Terry's palms were sweaty and he was afraid he would drop the camera if he didn't do this quick. "Come here." Purred the preacher. Terry thought *fuck that* and began to bring the camera up.

The bathroom door opened at that moment causing Terry to abort the photo and a man stepped half way inside. The intruder turned around to address someone on the other side of the bar. He spoke in a booming baritone "Wait. No, I said I was coming. Just wait for me. Gotta take a shit."

Terry was paralyzed with panic, but Eli reached forward and grabbed him by the hem of his jeans. "Shut the door," he whispered and Terry did. Outside the stall the door closed and the big man ambled into the room. Terry felt the preacher reaching for his belt buckle.

Passing the stall the big man pounded his fist on the wall producing a booming matched by his voice "Sorry fellas, I'm about to stink up the joint." He let a preamble fart fly and giggled, opening the last stall. "Could take a while too," he added. Terry felt Eli reach inside his pants and squirmed in panic, but Brother Eli seemed to think it was fun and insisted his hand under the elastic band of his underwear.

"Sure picked a classy spot for a hookup," said the big man, working his own trousers down. Terry heard the belt buckle clink on the tile floor. Terry's pants were slipping and he spread his stance wide to keep them up, afraid he wouldn't be able to get them fastened for his inevitable flight from the john. Eli ignored him and wrestled Terry's prick out of his pants. All the struggling had produced a semi-erect state for Terry and this encouraged Eli who leaned back and began to pump away with his right hand on himself and his left on Terry who moaned in terror.

There was a terrific rip and splash from the third stall and the big man groaned in satisfaction. Terry's senses were overloaded and threatening to overwhelm him. He looked down and saw that he was now fully erect and that Eli's concentration was total.

With his right hand he brought the camera up and tried to frame a shot, but the preacher's flailing hand and his own bouncing member kept blocking Eli's face from view. He leaned back against the door for a better shot.

Another loud fart echoed through the room and the big man chuckled. "Whew, sorry fellas."

Terry pressed the button and a bright flash blinded him. Eli's eyes were closed and he hadn't noticed, but the big man had.

"What're you doin in there?"

Terry was panicked, but determined to get the job done. No way in hell he was going through this without getting what he came for. He pointed the camera at the preacher's face and snapped another photo.

"You guys taking pictures?" came the big man's voice.

Brother Eli's eyes snapped open just in time to be incapacitated by Terry furiously snapping pictures and shattering the darkness with the strobe of Cal's fancy motor camera. The preacher shrieked and stood up.

"Hey, what's going on?" came from the crapping man's stall.

Eli tried to pull up his pants, but Terry punched him in the stomach, stealing his breath to cry out. He brought his knee up into the evangelist's face and the man crumpled onto the toilet.

"Everybody okay over there?" asked the big man. Terry put the camera back in his waistband and began to get his pants right again. Brother Eli was getting his wind back slowly, but the fight had gone out of him and he spent all his energy on crying. Great sucking sobs began to issue from him. Terry finished with his pants and grabbed the preacher. He held the man's head up and looked into his red face. His hands were already balled in tight fists. He struck the evangelist on the jaw. The minister went slack and Terry hit him again.

"Hey! What's going on over there?"

He switched hands and struck the preacher on the other side of his face. He clenched that fist hard as he could and did it again.

The big man began to buckle his own pants audibly and fumble with the latch on the stall.

"Faggots better not be doing what I think you're doing. I know the owner."

Terry opened the door and walked out. He didn't meet his own eyes in the mirror as he left.

He pulled open the door and walked straight and purposefully toward the door. He felt all eyes on him and didn't look at anyone else. Behind him he heard the big man making the discovery of Brother Eli in the stall. The deep rumbling of his voice rang out: "Aw fuck." Then Terry heard the door opening and the big voice command, "Hey, stop that asshole."

Terry doubled his pace as everyone turned to watch him. The big voice repeated his command and Terry heard the man moving in his direction. One guy half stepped into his path. Terry danced toward his interceptor and slammed his forehead into the middle of the man's face. He felt the nose give and heard several ugly pops as the man slumped to the floor. Terry broke into a run and reached the door.

Outside, Cal was parked across the street in his truck. When the door burst open, Terry was running full speed toward the pickup and jumped into the bed rather than take the time to circle around to the cab's passenger side.

Behind him a collection of queers filed out and gave short-lived pursuit as Cal fishtailed down the street and disappeared into the night.

The engine sound woke Irm up.

Shit. She hadn't meant to fall asleep. Wanted to wait in the house, but wasn't sure how she'd handle the dog, so she'd opted so stake out the place from her own vehicle. It had started to rain, and after a couple of hours, the soft, insistent thudding had put her under.

Now, she saw the pickup pull out of the drive and watched the tail lights recede from view. Fuck it, she didn't want to wait here any longer. Irm took the Glock from the dashboard and slipped it under her thigh as she started the engine.

She turned the wiper blades on, but kept the headlights off, and caught her reflection in the rearview. The bruise in the corner of her eye looked much darker in the green glow of the dashboard.

I'm a Fujiyama Mama and I'm just about to blow my top.

Irm cranked up the Wanda Jackson song, winked at her reflection and sang along with the Queen of Rockabilly.

And when I start erupting nobody gonna make me stop.

CHAPTER ELEVEN

MONDALE

Bob Musil sat across the booth from him and shook his head. "First I've heard of it." Mondale looked closely at his deputy, but couldn't find any reason to doubt him.

"This has got to be contained. I need to know any time Chowder's name or my own, for that matter, comes up." The State's Attorney's office hadn't had any more official contact with the Hamilton County Sheriff's Department that Mondale knew of. He thought the young lawyer might be shaking the branches, just hoping for something to fall, so Jimmy'd held his breath and not brought anyone into the loop about the investigation. He didn't want to send ripples through the system that might make him look nervous.

Musil was his obvious first contact and was claiming ignorance as far as the ASA's interest in the sheriff's office went. Bob had spent twenty years with the force in Castle Rock, Colorado before relocating to Spruce. His wife's bronchitis was cited as the primary reason for their move. The high altitude trapped the pollution from Denver and the mountains created a basin for the smog to settle in. It was hell on her respiratory system and they'd traded the dry, dirty climate for the muggy, but clean air of the Ozark region.

Mondale'd run virtually unopposed for his office three terms in a row, though he was aware of Bob Musil's attractiveness to some community elements as a candidate. He knew because Bob told him flat out. Came by his office and told Jimmy to his face that he'd been approached by some business leaders about the prospect of running for sheriff, but he'd turned them down. His goal in Missouri was to be the best number two Jimmy ever had. At first Mondale'd been unsure how to take the directness of his deputy, but over time had come to trust Musil with the most sensitive aspects of his job and office and the deputy had not proved unworthy of any trust or task Jimmy had yet given him.

"If you want my opinion, I'd say he's messing with you. He's an opportunist looking for a big score. Probably doing the same thing with a half dozen other weak leads. Hunches. Just playing the odds."

Jimmy shrugged. "Yeah. Occurred to me too." He took another sip of coffee. It had turned cold and was unpleasant. "But still. Got my attention. Keep a sharp lookout."

Musil nodded. "Will do."

"'Course that goes for Irma Thompson and Tate Dill or anybody else related to Chowder or Darlin's."

"Sure thing. If you want me to, I'll talk to my contacts in Jeff City, see what they've heard about Jordan."

Mondale shook his head. "No, not yet anyhow. If he's just making splashes, he'll be looking for ripples coming back his way. I don't want to give him any reason to keep looking our direction."

"Alright."

Etta Sanderson stopped at their table and refilled the coffee. "Sheriff, you look fresh," she said and smiled at him.

Bob's head tilted slightly as he reevaluated his boss. "She's right, Jimmy. You look good. Been exercising?"

Mondale winked at Etta. "Pleasure seeing you is all, Etta."

"Bull. But you go ahead and say so. Tell anybody you like, Jimmy Mondale. Maybe folks will start talking."

"They might at that," he agreed as she cleared their plates and walked them back to the kitchen.

Musil arched his eyebrows at him. "Anything I oughtta know?"

Mondale's radio crackled and he reached for it, ignoring his deputy's look. "Yeah, Wanda, go ahead." He said.

"Sheriff," came the voice on the other end, "There's an accident out on Buisness 71. Fatalities."

"Shit," he said under his breath. Then into the radio, "Who's on it?"

"Highway Patrol is on the scene, but I thought you'd want to know about it."

"Thanks, Wanda. I'm on my way." Bob Musil was already standing and paying the bill. Jimmy tipped his imaginary hat to Etta as he headed out the door.

The bend in the road was nasty. There were fatalities on that stretch more often than any other in Spruce if not Hamilton County. Last night's rain would've created dangerous conditions to compound the already treacherous curves. It wouldn't have taken much to send some poor soul off the road.

As Mondale pulled up to the scene, he nodded at the Highway Patrolman. He racked his brain for the kid's name and settled on Gil, but wasn't sure if it was his first or last name. Getting out of his car and shutting the door with both hands, he decided either would do fine. "Gil."

"Sheriff."

"What've we got?"

Gil led him over the tell tale tire marks going round the bend in the road and right off to the lip of the hill where the tow truck was backed up and dangling its cable down to a pickup truck that was twisted around a large Bull Pine.

Mondale whistled low when he saw the wreckage. "Who

found it?"

Gil answered without looking away from the bent truck. "Fisherman. Climbed down, but they were already dead."

"They?"

"Girl and a dog."

"Jesus."

"Yeah." Gil looked at Mondale. "Missouri tags, but long expired. Used to be registered to a Terrence Hickerson in Hamilton County."

Mondale looked back at the truck. "Really?"

"Yeah. Know him?"

"Know who he is, yeah. Woman though, huh?"

"Yeah, young. Blonde. Know her?"

Mondale shook his head. "Huh-uh." Below, the driver searched for a place to secure his tow cable and Mondale clapped Officer Gil on the shoulder. "Lemme know if they find any I.D. on her. I'm headed over to Hickerson's place."

"Alright. Hey, Sheriff?" Mondale turned. "It's probably nothing, but," Gil lowered his voice and stepped toward Mondale who followed suit and inclined his head for privacy.

"What?"

"Assistant State's Attorney, name of Jordan has been requesting information about Spruce and Hamilton County. Asking about bike traffic and stuff." Mondale went cold. "I only mention it 'cause he asked about you too. Seemed interested in you for some reason. Thought you'd want to know."

Mondale held out his hand and Gil took it. They shook firmly and Mondale said, "Thanks. Not sure what that's all about, but I appreciate it."

"No problem, Sheriff. I'll let you know when we identify the driver."

Mondale got into his car. "Do that."

TERRY

Cal had driven them back to his Aunt Jeannette's house where Terry'd gone straight to his liquor supply and damn near emptied it. Cal watched his friend and business partner finish off three near empty bottles of whiskey before taking any himself. He'd driven home watching his rearview the whole way for anybody who might be following them. Branson was more than an hour's drive through the winding roads and Terry had waited twenty minutes before pounding on the glass for him to pull over and let him into the cab. It had begun to rain and the muggy clime was only intensified by it. Cal blasted the air conditioner to keep from smothering in the heavy air outside.

Cal had looked at Terry expectantly and got the message, in no uncertain terms, that he was not to say word one until he was spoken to. Terry stared sullenly out the window at nothing in particular. There was a cut and a bruise forming on his forehead and the knuckles on both his hands were beginning to swell, making it difficult to hold the camera tight, but he clutched it to his chest like a baby he'd birthed.

Terry had eventually passed out on the floor still holding Cal's camera in one hand and an empty bottle in the other. When he woke up he was alone in the front room of Jeanette's place. According to Cal the old bat hardly ever came out of her bedroom except to trip on the rug on the way to the kitchen once in a while. There were large wet spots on his shirt and pants that gave off sharp, acrid odors and didn't mix too well. He stumbled into the kitchen and vomited proper. He managed to empty himself mostly into the sink and turned on the faucet to rinse it down. Then he bent over and put his head beneath the water flow. He rubbed his face vigorously and turned his mouth up to drink.

After he'd drunk his fill and spit most of the puke flavor out of his mouth, he unzipped and peed in Jeanette's sink. He was shaking off when Cal came in from the other room.

"Shit Terry, c'mon. You know where the can is."

"I don't believe you have any place being upset with me, man. I believe you should get on your knees and kiss my ass for what I did for us last night."

"So?"

"Gold."

Cal clapped his hands. "Hot damn. Let's get it printed."

Terry held his hand up. "I'll see to that."

"No, c'mon, Terry. It's my camera."

"And it's my dick, so shut the fuck up." Cal's eyes widened, but before he could say anything, Terry cut him off. "I said 'shut the fuck up.'"

Cal drove them back to Terry's place. Eventually they were heading out to Cuba where Cal had a contact he wanted to use to develop the pictures. Terry had no problem with that idea. The thought of a stranger handling the sensitive material didn't sound too smart.

When they pulled up into his driveway, something struck Terry as odd, but he couldn't put a finger to that particular mental itch just then. He opened the door and went toward his bedroom for a change of clothes, having leaked a variety of digestive fluids onto his current outfit during the course of the night. He stripped naked and hopped into the shower and jumped when the cold blast of water hit him. Warming it up took too long, so he took cold showers when he was in a hurry, which he was most of the times he decided he could stand to bathe.

Stepping out, he stood dripping onto the dirty shirt he'd left on the floor and reached for the clean one he'd brought with him to the bathroom to dry off with before slipping it over his head. Then he bent over the sink and squeezed water out of the handfuls of hair he could grab. Next he put on a different pair of jeans and the same socks he'd worn the night before.

He stopped at the fridge and poked through its contents: ketchup, Vess Grape soda, a Kentucky Fried Chicken bag (which he grabbed), and three cans of Stag (which he pocketed). As he was about to leave he remembered to scoop some dry dog food for Layla into her dish and called out to her that breakfast was ready. He was mildly surprised she hadn't come to see him yet, but figured she was out in the woods somewhere gnawing on a root or a squirrel skull.

When he climbed back into Cal's truck, feeling a thousand percent better, he tossed the driver a can of Stag and cracked one for himself. Cal wheeled them out of the drive and they were on the highway five minutes later. Twenty minutes after that, Terry looked at Cal and said, "Where the hell was my truck?"

CHOWDER

His cell phone was about to vibrate itself right off the dresser and all the loose change and his keys, resting atop, were buzzing along with it. Sounded like a bee-hive rolling down a gravel road. He turned over and grabbed it. Hettie was moaning beside him, "Fuck's sake, Chowder, turn it off." His fingers were clumsy with sleep and he couldn't operate the tiny buttons. He squeezed it and jabbed at the controls randomly until it stopped humming. Holding it flat against his face he barked, "What?"

Tate Dill's voice answered. "Sorry Chowder, I just wanted to make sure everything was alright."

Chowder sat up straight and Hettie pulled the covers he'd displaced back over her. "What's going on?"

"You weren't here when I came in this morning."

"At the shop?"

"Yeah."

"Where's Irm?"

"Not here."

"Who's with you?"

"That's what I'm saying. Place was empty when I came in. Doors unlocked, lights on, but nobody home."

"Fuck."

"Just wanted –"

He hung up on Tate. He dialed his daughter's number as he strode naked out of his bedroom into the front of the house. The patient chirping of the ring tone aggravated him as he split the blinds on the front window and peeked outside. Nobody there.

Irm's voicemail picked up and Chowder growled, "Call me back. Now." He went to the kitchen and opened the refrigerator. He reached in for a glass of black coffee brewed yesterday and left to cool overnight. He palmed two peeled hardboiled eggs and popped them into his mouth, washing them down with the coffee. Back in the bedroom, Hettie murmured inquisitively and he said, "If you see or hear from Irm, call me."

He slid into his jeans without underwear, careful to tuck himself well into them before zipping up, and grabbed a long t-shirt. He bent forward to lace his boots over his swollen feet and grunted with the effort of reaching them while his hair hung gray and greasy in his eyes. With one hand he pushed it backward over the top of his head and instinctively made the motion to tie it into a tail, though it hadn't been long enough to do so in a decade.

He slipped into his leather jacket and kicked open the front door tapping a Camel between his lips. Climbing into the cab of his truck, he paused to light it and crawled under the steering wheel with minimal effort. He started the engine, flipped the cell phone open again and dialed the shop.

Tate answered on the third ring. "Anything missing?"

"Not that I can tell. Office was locked up and the safe wasn't touched. Cash drawer was empty, but I found it all inside the safe. I'm doing an inventory now, but don't see anything obvious."

"Call me if you do."

He hung up and called Darlin's. Big Randy answered. "Hey."

"Irm around there?"

"Nah. Haven't seen her all night."

"How'd we do last night?"

Randy made an audible shrug. "Meh, average."

"Lemme know if you see Irm."

He pulled off the paved road onto a private gravel drive and disappeared into the wild. The tangle of trees created an immediate green canopy completely enveloping him and the narrow road twisted sharply with large chunks of rock and rotted tree stumps pocking the way. The path rose and fell continually and sometimes dropped away completely at the edges. His speed dipped to an average of fifteen miles an hour and he followed the aimless trail for ten minutes, fording a trickle of a creek and passing over a narrow wooden bridge, before pulling over to a cleared shoulder and exiting.

From the glove box, he removed his Colt and held it loosely in his right hand as he headed up the hill he'd parked beside. The ground was loose here and there and he had to use his left hand to grip sapling trunks and pull himself up. At the crest, he paused, looking down on the small cabin's back-side.

The windows were covered from the inside. A septic tank was rusting in the back yard and the satellite dish mounted on the roof looked like it could be knocked over with a thrown rock. Nothing moved around the cabin and after a moment, Chowder descended the hill toward it.

The wood porch creaked loudly when he hefted himself upon it and the wood groaned with each step approaching the front door. He opened it and the hinges took up announcing him where the porch left off. Inside, the wood floors were scuffed and dusty and a single bare bulb hung from the ceiling, illuminating the room.

From the kitchen he heard a scraping movement that stopped abruptly a second later. Chowder called out, "Who we got in here?" as he moved toward the kitchen and the sound. The smell inside was worse than any lock-up he'd ever visited. The harsh chemical odor seared his nostrils, and he wiped at the corners of his eyes.

The kitchen was lit with two long fluorescent bulbs, each at half strength, that seemed only to illuminate the dirt worked into the yellow tile of the floor. A green Formica table with dull metal legs was pushed up against the yellowed refrigerator and covered with crumpled squares of tinfoil and burn marks. A dirty yardbird Tate had hired was sleeping on the floor beneath the table, a white cake of dried spit flecking the five-day growth of his beard. Chowder kicked the table and knocked over an empty two-liter pop bottle. It bounced on the grimy tile next to his hip. The passed out shit-scab hardly twitched.

Chowder walked over to the sink and filled a chipped glass he found on the counter with tap water. He splashed the man's face with it, but did not wake him. Instead a dark stain began to spread from the crotch of his already questionably marked jeans. "Shit's sake," muttered Chowder, then he went to the basement stairway.

Going down the narrow wooden stairway, Chowder leaned heavily on the rail, which bowed between supports with every step. In the basement the lab was clean and orderly in the middle of the room, with a border of junk strewn along the walls. There was a four foot cleared path around the work area and he walked all the way around it, absently inspecting the scene for anything out of place. Twice around and everything seemed in order. Chowder headed back upstairs.

In the kitchen, he opened the refrigerator and removed the big plastic tub of instant coffee crystals. He unscrewed the lid and took a big whiff. Dunkin' Donuts had ruined the cheap shit for him permanently, but if he made it triple strength, he should be able to choke it down.

The electric coffee maker was coated with a brown film that didn't rinse away in the sink, but he made a pot anyway. While it was brewing, he stood near the machine trying to dislodge the crank-house smell from his nose, but the alternative the instant crystals offered was a weak and flimsy one that dissolved into the astringent atmosphere without a trace.

As it brewed, Chowder checked his cell phone. Reception was spotty in the area and he thought perhaps he'd missed a call from Tate or Het, but he had not. The passed-out asshole on the floor began to mumble something, then sat up like a switch had flipped, choking and gagging on some phantom irritant. He passed through three distinct stages of panic in five seconds, before his demonic twitching dissipated, and he gazed up, reasonably sober, at Chowder.

Chowder poured a cup for himself in a green mug with a logo for Chowder's Bait 'N More chipping and fading away on the side. He grimaced through the first sip and stared back at the man on the floor. "Pissed yourself."

The man blinked again, then looked down at the wet spot on his jeans. "The hell are you?" he asked.

Chowder ignored the question and instead fired back one of his own. "Who's watching the shop?"

"Huh?"

"Don't tell me you're in charge, here."

"I was jus-"

Chowder splashed the steaming coffee in the dirtbag's face.

The man screamed and threw his hands up defensively too late. He swiped at the scalding liquid, throwing it to the floor in tiny splashes.

"Shit, fuck. Shit. Fuck. Shit." The yardbird reached the far end of his vocabulary and circled back. "Fuck, shit. Fuck."

Chowder poured himself another cup of coffee. He reached over the top of the man's head toward one of the squares of tin foil with a trace of powder left in a crease. He dumped the powder into his coffee and swished the liquid around before tasting it. His phone rang and he took one more sip of the coffee before setting the mug back on the counter and reaching into his pocket. He saw Irm's number appear on the screen and answered. "Bout time."

"You called?"

"Don't start. Get your ass out to the cabin."

"Thought I was fired."

"You got a mess to clean up." He closed the phone and looked at the man on the floor. This was exactly the variety of shit that he didn't need in his life anymore. He made up his mind about a few things right then.

CHAPTER TWELVE

TERRY

Cal took them to a house in an old neighborhood. In Cuba there weren't other kinds. The place was sturdy looking and neat. Terry distrusted it immediately. "You sure about this dude?"

"Oh yeah. Used to teach school and shit, but not anymore."

"No?"

"Nah. Runs a fence through a pawnshop now. Cleans money some, and still does photography stuff."

"How'd you meet him again?"

"Pawned some shit. Got to talking."

Cal killed the engine and the front door of the house opened. A man in his late forties, thinning brown hair swept back and wire-rimmed glasses giving his face a harmless quality. He raised his arm to Cal and opened his door. "C'mon."

Terry followed Cal up the steps to the front porch and shook hands with the man who Cal introduced as Frank. Frank had them come inside and offered something to drink.

Cal said he could go for an iced tea when the options were given and Terry shook his head. Inside it was as clean and tasteful as out. Terry wondered at the dark wood furniture and clear windows letting the abundant sunlight in at slanty angles. A tabby cat dozed in a sunspot on a chair parked near an oak dining table. The house smelled fresh too, like chicken pot-pie and vanilla. Terry's unease grew.

Frank brought Cal his iced tea in a glass with a wedge of lemon in the top and Cal accepted it, smiling broadly, thanking his host. "So," said Frank, "You've got something for me?"

Cal took a gulp of the tea and nodded. "Yep. Got some film we need developed. Can't take it to one of those one-hour places, but we do need it real quick."

Frank nodded like this was a normal day for him. "Sure. Well, usually it's a hundred for a roll, but you get the friend rate. Seventy-five."

"Dollars?" said Terry.

Frank nodded. "My time is worth that."

"The hell, man?" Terry looked at Cal.

"Dude," Cal assured Terry. "Frank is good. This is a good deal."

"Says you."

"Think about it. This isn't the kind of thing you can just slip the kid at Walgreens twenty bucks to do. Frank's..." he searched for the right word, "Discreet."

Frank nodded and held his hand out for the camera that Terry still guarded close to his chest. "That's a nice looking camera you have, Mr. Hickerson. Can I see it?"

Terry gave Frank his best hard stare, but the affable expression never changed and he finally handed it over. "Mmm," said Frank, accepting the camera. "Image is everything, huh?"

Cal snorted. "I picked that one up from you, remember?"

"Oh yes," said Frank. "Said you needed one with a motor and high speed shutter." He raised his eyebrows. "Let's see how we did."

MONDALE

Terry Hickerson's house looked abandoned. The tarp serving as the east wall on the southern room was frayed and faded. He peeled it back and called for Terry. The fragrance of the room was mildew and bacon grease. "Hickerson. You there?"

He pounded on the front door thinking there was a good chance that Terry was sleeping off a drunk. When he tried the knob, he found it unlocked. "Terry, door's open, I'm coming in." It was dark inside though there was no covering on the windows. Scratch marks on the floor and the layer of fine brown hair coating the couch caught his eye and he remembered Gil saying there'd been a dog killed in the accident, too. Shame.

He toured the shack and found it unoccupied, though there were dirty, wet clothes on the bathroom floor and water still on the walls of the shower.

His radio crackled and Bob Musil's voice asked for his forty. Mondale left by the front door and circled around the back of the house. He answered Musil. "I'm at the Hickerson house. Nobody here. Anybody seen him yet?" The side of the house featured a large unorganized wood-pile, which, aside from housing a nest of yellow jackets, Jimmy figured, heated the home. There'd been a wood burning stove in the front room, he recalled, though in the winter the shack must stink to hell, because the pieces of scrap and tree branches collected here were wet and rotting. Some of them had once been furniture and there was even a disintegrating cork-board sticking out of the middle of the heap.

Musil came back. "Negative. We've got a bulletin out. We'll find him."

The grass was up to his knees and the ground full of holes and mounds. He picked carefully through it, stooping to duck jutting branches from a walnut tree leaning on the roof. He scratched his cheek on a branch and cursed as he rounded the corner of the house. "Roger. Who's on now?"

"We got Townsend just coming on."

"Send him out. I'm going to stick around till he shows up. I want to speak to Hickerson just as soon as he pops up." There was a brick barbeque pit sticking out of the overgrown lawn in the back. Mondale poked through the old ashes, finding the edges of burnt garbage and pop cans. From beneath a half melted forty ounce Styrofoam cup a spider scurried for the cover of an unraveled Pringles canister and the sheriff kicked a cement block over revealing a deep wet rut where worms and roly-polys socialized.

"Roger that. I need to see you soon as you can get back here, Jim."

"Sure. Send Townsend out and I'll see you in a jiff." He put the radio back on his hip and looked around the back yard. He moved toward a rusted tool shed with a half open sliding door. Inside it smelled of gasoline, oil and wet grass, though the lawn mower was buried in the lawn and he couldn't imagine when it had last been cut. Garden tools that had once belonged to Terry Hickerson's father sat on shelves and hung on nails in the wall and he casually inventoried the collection.

He wondered what Musil needed to talk to him about. Officer Gil's confirmation of Dennis Jordan's looking into him was consuming his thoughts. It irritated him and distracted everything else he was processing. He needed to talk with Chowder soon, but he couldn't afford to be seen talking to him any more.

What bothered him most at the moment was something Musil had said. He'd called him 'Jim.' Not 'Jimmy,' not 'sheriff,' just 'Jim.' He didn't like the sound of that.

CHOWDER

Irm arrived at the cabin huffing. Chowder watched her crest the hill and then awkwardly descend. The physical effort broke down some of her attitude. When she reached him, he gestured for her to sit with him on the porch, which she was obliged to do. They sat in silence for a moment while she caught her breath. He dug at the skin under his fingernails and dabbed some blood off his arms with his t-shirt.

"The fuck did you go last night?"

"Had something to do."

"Hey. Look at me."

She did and the way her feet dangled from the porch, Chowder saw her as a petulant grade-schooler again, trying to prove something to the whole world and him most of all.

"Do what I fucking say."

Irm's eyes rolled and she looked away.

"Think I'm kidding?" He stared hard at her until she shook her head slowly. "Need to know that I can count on you." He gestured toward the horizon as if to take in the whole world. "Who else do I have? Your mom? She ain't gonna be around forever. Sheriff? He ain't like us. Tate? He ain't blood." She looked at his knees. "Can I count on you or should I fold up shop?"

"You serious?"

Chowder nodded. "Getting old."

"I keep noticing."

Chowder didn't quite smile. "Got a good arrangement with the sheriff here. Could maybe pass that on." He raised his eyebrows slightly. "But I need to be sure."

"Okay."

"Partnership. Mondale has to be sure too."

"I don't like him."

"I know. He knows. Liking's got less to do with it than you think."

She nodded slowly.

"Can you?"

She nodded more definitely, then whispered, "Yeah."

"What?"

"I said, 'yes.'"

"Okay then." He struggled to stand. "First order of business: help me stand up." She hopped off the porch, climbed the stair and offered her father her arm. He grabbed it and together they put him upright. He winced at the contact. There were some nasty scratches on his arms. "Next." He motioned with a nod of his head for her to follow him inside.

When they entered the kitchen, Irm took in the scene. The table was turned over and a pair of legs in dirty jeans stuck out on the far side of it. She walked around to get a better look at the body.

"Know its name?" Chowder asked.

"Dale something," she answered. "Tate knew him from Jeff City."

"Yeah well, I'm gonna talk to Tate about that."

"Happened?"

"Had to be let go."

Irm looked at the bloody scratches on Chowder's arms. "Why didn't you just shoot?"

Chowder cocked his head sideways. "C'mon, Irma." He took a deep whiff of the room. "Same reason I ain't gonna smoke a cigarette or use the stove in here. Which reminds me, get a new coffee maker. That one?" He gestured at the counter, "is disgusting."

She nodded, and took a closer look at Dale something. One of his front teeth was dangling into his mouth by a gory thread. His nose was flattened to his skull and blood trails snaked out of what was left of the nostrils, running into the cracks and spaces between the tile underneath him. His throat was caved in and purplish. "What'd you use?"

Chowder just held up his right fist and mimed punching someone on the ground. "Need you to clean this up."

When he left Irm to bury Dale something in the woods and clean up the kitchen, she seemed to be in a better mood. He got back in his truck and once he was out on the main road, opened his cell and called the store.

Tate picked up. "It's me," Chowder announced. "How're things looking?"

"Fine. Kinda busy this morning."

"I'm on my way."

He hung up and called Hettie at home. When she answered he said, "Found her."

"Thank Christ. You take off your belt?"

"We talked."

"I hope to hell you did more than that."

"Made her clean up some shit."

"Wait till I see her."

"Need you to come into the shop."

"Now?"

"Yeah, Tate says it's busy."

"Where're you?"

"I'm coming in, too."

"Why you need me then?"

"I'm firing Tate when I get there." There was a beat of silence on Hettie's end. "It's gotta be done. I've decided."

"I'm on my way."

TERRY

The trip back from Cuba started in uncomfortable silence. Cal was right. Frank was good and paying him to develop the pictures in private was worth it. There were some very usable images printed. When he'd seen them, Terry'd frozen up. Cal was agog. He'd taken each print in turn, his jaw dropping and eyes watering.

Frank seemed pleased with the work and didn't ask any questions.

Cal had thanked Frank profusely and shook his hand. He'd cracked jokes, self-consciously filling in all the awkward gaps in the conversation. But when they were alone in the truck even Cal was at a loss.

Anybody looking to identify Eli would be able to tell it was the preacher working both cocks. Two of the shots even showed Eli with his mouth wrapped around Terry, but for the life of him, Terry couldn't remember that. Cal had paid the seventy-five bucks out of his own pocket, agreeing that

Terry'd done all the heavy lifting on this one. After twenty minutes of silence, Cal tried to console his friend.

"Hey, nobody's ever gonna know it's you. Hell, other than us and Frank and that preacher, ain't any reason for anybody else to even see em. Ever. And plus, the angle and all?" He looked to Terry to see if he was following, "Makes your dick look big, man."

Terry didn't respond.

"Seriously."

Terry saw a convenience mart and liquor store up ahead. "Pull over."

Cal did. Nervously, he looked at his partner. "What're you thinking?"

Terry started to root through the glove compartment and the trash on the floor. He found a pistol and a plastic bag and handed them to Cal.

"Hoah, Terry, c'mon man, think about this. We've hit these guys before."

Terry pulled a pocket-knife out of his jeans. "You owe me this. I need to do this. Gotta…" He wasn't sure how to finish the thought.

"Okay, okay, okay. Hold on, lemme see –"

"You my partner?"

"Hey, Terry, man, you know it."

"Back me up."

Terry had taken his arms out and pulled his t-shirt up to cover his face like a ninja mask. He was out of the cab, across the lot and through the front door before Cal could think. He put his head inside the plastic bag and gouged eyeholes, checked his gun and followed.

The dude behind the counter didn't look up when Terry came through the door. He was busy bagging some liquor for the old lady writing a check at the register. He did a quick scan of the store and counted two other customers, but no one he immediately took to be a threat. Too late anyway. He was climbing over the counter and pushing the cashier's head onto its surface already.

"Open it." He said. The cashier was crying and struggling to get the register open with his left hand, while Terry touched the skin beneath his left eye with the tip of the blade. The woman buying the liquor looked at Terry and frowned. "Shut up," Terry cut her off before she could say anything.

From the back of the store he heard a woman gasp and drop her purchase. She moved in blind flight for the door. Just as she reached it, Cal came in, bag over his head and pistol raised. He pointed it right in the lady's face and she shrieked. Cal held his finger up to his lips to shush her. "Back up, now." He said. He moved her toward the back of the store and grabbed the cowboy too. When they were safely in place standing against the beer cooler, Cal called out "Clear."

"Get that bitch open," Terry yelled. He let the cashier stand to operate the register and in a second the drawer popped with a *ping*. "Get a sack." The cashier pulled a plastic bag out and fluffed it open. "Put the money in it." He did so, sobbing under his breath. "And shut up with that crying. Makin' me sick over here."

The old lady meanwhile had bent over her checkbook and been scrawling away. She looked up at the cashier and said, "Can I get cash back?"

"Hoah shit! That was intense." Cal pounded the steering wheel as they tore ass out of the parking lot. He looked sideways at Terry whose black mood had indeed lifted. A little adrenaline was always good for his sour patches. "How much?"

Terry was looking behind them, but no one was following. "Better take a different route back."

"You think?" Cal made some quick mental adjustments. "How much, already?"

Terry opened the paper bag and began organizing the handful of green bills. "Not too much, partner."

"Fuck it. Who cares? Feels good."

"Yeah. Guess it does." Terry decided not to count it yet.

With his head proper cleared, he felt he was able to address their blackmail enterprise. "Alrighty, what's the plan for these pictures?"

Cal settled down a bit. He was glad his partner was leveled off by the jack they'd just pulled, and he was glad he seemed ready to talk directly about the pictures and what the forward course of action would be, but he didn't exactly trust Terry's mood to stay balanced long. He'd have to proceed cautiously. Try not to make the wrong jokes. On the other hand, don't let Terry catch you being careful, 'cause that's likely to set him off, too. "Well, shit, I figure we mail em to him at the TV station with a note. Maybe a place to make a payment drop."

During the heist, Cal had grabbed a six-pack from the fridge. Now Terry popped the tabs on two, giving one to Cal, and taking a big blast from his own.

"Huh. Not bad. But how do we make sure that nobody else opens up the pictures? We don't wanna let more people in. Complicate it," Terry said, taking a swig from a warm Stag. "So how you figure we go about making contact with the preacher?"

Cal took a drink and focused on the road. "Shit, kemosabe, I'd say you already did that."

Terry stopped drinking and glared at Cal, but his hard look didn't last. He cracked a smile that leaked beer down his chin, then choked on the swallow he'd been working on. He felt foam burning his nostrils and wiped his mouth and nose with his shirt.

Cal smiled. Good to have his friend back.

MONDALE

When Townsend pulled up outside the Hickerson house, Mondale was sitting on the slanted front porch intently smoking a cigarette. He nodded at the deputy and stood, getting the pops out of his knees and back.

Townsend got out of his car and came across the lawn to meet Jimmy. He looked spooked. "What's the matter, deputy?"

Townsend wouldn't look at his face. "Musil says you'd better get back to the station straight away."

"I was planning on it. What's going on?"

"He wants to talk to you."

"Kinda figured that, son. You know what about?"

Townsend shook his head and looked at the ground. "Think you'd better talk to Bob."

"Kid, don't get squirrelly on me."

"No, sir."

Jimmy was uneasy, but decided it would be better to deal with Musil face to face than this kid who looked like he might puke if he were asked any more questions. "Fine. You know Terry Hickerson by sight?"

Townsend shook his head.

"Well he's the only shitbird likely to come around anyway. He runs with a guy named Dotson. Big ol' boy, thin red hair. Hickerson's a skinny runt and he's likely to be jumpy. Wouldn't put it past him to be packing either, so try not to make him nervous. Let him know I need to see him down at the station. He gives you any trouble, you let me know."

Townsend nodded.

"You hear me?"

"Yes, sir."

"Alright. Relax, would you? You're making me nervous." Jimmy got into his car and started it up. He radioed Wanda at the station to let her know he was on his way.

Her voice came back choked and tight. "Okay, Sheriff."

Shit, thought Jimmy. This was gonna be bad.

CHOWDER

When he got to the store, he could see that it had been a busy afternoon. Either the rain and mist from the night before or, more likely, some unaccountable herd instinct he'd given up on second guessing over the years put folks in a fishing frame of mind. Bait, pussy or crank, it didn't matter, there were unseen forces driving the market. Retail. Shit.

Tate looked up from the register where he was restocking cigarettes. "Jeez, Chowder, you missed a rush."

"Hettie showed up yet?"

"Yeah, she's in the office, prepping the deposit."

Chowder crossed behind the counter and to the office. He opened the door and found his wife sorting through stacks of cash separated into denominations, little piles of coins and an unruly handful of credit card receipts. "You settle that batch yet?"

"Just did," she answered without looking up.

"Alright. Leave the rest. I'm gonna need to do this now."

"Okay, I'll be right out."

Chowder walked toward the back door and called for Tate to follow him. When he'd unlocked it he waited for Tate to catch up. Tate arrived with a neatly tied thirty-three gallon trash bag twenty seconds later.

"Figured I'd grab this while we were headed toward the dumpster." Chowder rolled his eyes as he watched the little douchebag heave the trash into the refuse bin.

When Tate turned around, Chowder broke his nose with right jab.

"You're fired, Tate. Come around any more, I'll have to kick your ass."

"Wha tha fa?" Tate managed through the bloody fingers covering his mouth, but Chowder had already shut the door behind him, and he was left standing alone in back of the bait shop.

MONDALE

When Jimmy arrived at the station, it was midafternoon and the shift change had already happened. His day should be ending about now. On the drive over he'd already been making dinner plans in the back of his mind. Thinking about chancing by the grocery store again. Maybe he'd run into Julie. Could happen. He tried to think of something practical to pick up. Chicken breasts – make a salad with em. Or stir-fry it with some rice and broccoli. Something he'd never tried before. No more corn dogs.

But he was just trying to distract himself. Something unpleasant was waiting for him. Musil wanted to talk to him, to 'Jim.' Probably meant a personal issue. Work related, he'd have said 'Sheriff,' county stuff he might've said 'Jimmy.' But just 'Jim' indicated a personal issue. The familiar mixed with the formal in a way he just couldn't reconcile as harmless.

Something involving the ASA maybe. A complication with Chowder-related issues. Incident out at Darlin's or some meth bust not on the agreed-to schedule he and Chowder had set. Something messy like that, probably. Which meant his day wasn't really over. He'd probably be lucky to have the energy to heat up the rest of the corn dogs when he got home. Hell.

As he opened the station door his cell phone rang. Stepping through, he leaned on the reception desk to fish it out of his pocket. Wanda was getting ready to leave for the day and she gave him a worried look like she expected he was going to ask her to stay or had some unpleasant task in mind for her tomorrow. He got a hold of the phone, and the caller I.D. said it was Julie. How'd she have this number? He didn't remember giving it to her last night. Maybe she'd got it from Eileen some time before.

"Hey," he said. He smiled at Wanda and waved her on. She could go home, he'd just stopped there to answer his call. Wanda still looked nervous, but she made to leave at his gesture. She put her hand on his shoulder as she passed and he turned to watch her leave. She'd worked for him for seven years and she'd never touched him before.

Julie's voice answered, "Hey, yourself."

"How'd you get this number?"

"Oh, you think I'm stalking you?" There was mirth in her suggestion. This was good. Just what he needed, a little emotional pick-me-up to get through the rest of his long night.

"No, that's not what I meant. I just don't recall giving it

to you."

"Would you have?"

"'Course." Wanda turned to look at him through the front door from the parking lot. He waved and she returned it, if hesitantly. "What's going on?" He turned to head for his office.

"I really enjoyed dinner last night. Best corn dogs I've ever had."

"Well, thank you. I try," he whispered. His own voice sounded very loud in the station. He looked around and realized it was because no one else was speaking. In fact no one else was working. Everyone was looking at him.

"I was thinking maybe we could do it again?"

"Tonight?" It felt like everyone was listening in on his personal conversation.

"But you could come over to my place this time. I'd like to cook you dinner. You could bring some beers or something."

"Well that sounds nice actually, but I don't know if tonight's going to work."

"You're not afraid, are you, Jimmy?"

"Well." She was blunt. Realizing he was, in fact, not eager for anybody there to know who he was talking to, or about what, he turned around and cupped his mouth over the phone. "As an elected official, I have to be, a little bit."

"Bullshit, Jimmy. Come on over tonight. I won't take no for an answer."

He was simultaneously thrilled and appalled that she'd called him. On the one hand she was an attractive young woman whose company he enjoyed and on the other she was the same age as his own daughter and her forwardness raised some red flags for him.

Bob Musil stepped out of the break room and stood statue still, his arms folded across his chest and eyes locked on Jimmy. Mondale acknowledged him with a tilt of his chin and gave him a raised hand like he'd be right with him.

To Julie he said, "I might have to work."

"Really?"

"Something's come up. I'd love to say yes, but I'm afraid I'll have to call you back." He could feel her disappointment seeping through the phone and it pleased him and kept his own disappointment company. "But maybe." He sensed her brighten. "I'll just have to call you back."

"Alright."

He hung up and turned around. Nothing moved in the whole station. Everyone looked at him with earnest expressions of what? Had that little shit from Jeff City made some kind of public statement? Had the lawyer really learned something about his arrangement with Chowder? Learned about the whores and crank labs? The people they'd killed to keep gangsters out of Spruce? His staff looked shocked and ready to rush him.

"Jim, why don't you come in here and have a seat."

"What the hell, Bob?" He went into his office and Musil closed the door behind them. "What's going on?"

Musil stood at the door as if checking to make sure no one was listening outside. Then he turned to face Jimmy, but said nothing.

"Spit it out, Deputy. Stepping on my last nerve, here."

"I think you should sit, Jim."

"The hell you say."

"It's about the wrecked truck this morning."

That was a relief. Mondale's shoulders dropped as the tension left them and he pulled out the chair in front of him. As he began to sit an awful thought occurred to him, "Jesus, Bob. What's going on?"

"Jim, it's about Eileen."

"My Eileen?"

TERRY

It was near dark when they pulled up outside of Terry's house. "Where the hell did my truck go?" he said.

Cal shrugged. "Wendell take it for a joyride?"

That'd be the day. His boy was so timid, he needed permission to take a shit. "I hope so." Terry racked his brain to come up with a scenario in which his son might steal something from him. Sadly, it was beyond the scope of his imagination. Still, he could always hope. "If he did, I'll whup his butt."

At that moment, Deputy Townsend rolled up behind Cal and flashed the red and blues. "Shit!" they said in unison, and Terry closed the door he was about to get out of. Cal threw the truck into gear and dug a nice new rut through Terry's front lawn. "How the hell they find us so quick?" said Cal.

"Drive," urged Terry. He took the paper bag from the liquor store and stuffed it under the seat with the rest of the trash. Terry thought about the pictures in the envelope Frank had developed for them and looked around for a secure spot to stash them.

Cal clipped the passenger side mirror on a tree and Terry jumped as far as he could from the seat, bumping against the gear-shift as he did. Cal swung the wheel sharply to the left when he hit the tree and drove them through a hedge of bushes. There was a sudden lurch and Terry was picked up and thrown against the windshield.

The truck was stopped, the front passenger tire lodged in a rut and Terry's hip bone had caused a spider-web pattern to spread across the windshield. Cal's nose broke on the steering wheel and he was dripping blood all over the front of his shirt. Without another thought, Terry slid the manila envelope behind the front seat of the truck and waited for the cops to drag him out.

Deputy Townsend called out from behind the stalled truck. "Put your hands where I can see them. Hands up." Terry waited patiently for him, not particularly motivated to move this whole process along. How had they found them so quickly? He and Cal had held up dozens of places and never been arrested for any of them. They hadn't even hit a spot in town. Someone must've got the license number and called it in.

From the driver's side, Terry heard the policeman calling out instructions, but neither he nor Cal were listening to them. Cal was looking at him like he'd just woken up, his face painted in lipstick. The policeman's orders were arriving like shouting underwater. He thought maybe he'd just go to sleep.

PART II

The night shift was slow at the Maranatha Family Bookstore in Branson, so Gloria ventured out from behind the register and browsed the aisles and displays for any dusty spots, crooked or misplaced items. On her rounds she found plastic wrap stuffed between slots along the greeting card wall. Someone had helped themselves to a compact disc.

She unfolded the crinkled wrapping, shaking her head and wondering why anyone would steal religious merchandise. Not that it was uncommon, but it never failed to illicit surprise and a mixture of anger and sympathy for whatever poor, floundering soul was driven to display such good and bad spiritual sense at the same time. When the label on the packaging was legible she found that it was one of her favorites. Hmm, going way back. Sandi Patti. Classic. Oh well, maybe it would do them good, she thought.

Around the corner, she paused to straighten the endcap. The Brother Eli display was heavily perused she noticed. Books were laying open, face down, ruining the spines, CDs and VHS tapes had been browsed and carelessly returned and there was more trash lying on top. She straightened the display with quick, jerky motions as a probable culprit sprang to mind. A man in his late thirties, with a bolo tie and stone-washed jeans, wearing avi-

ator shades and a ton of cologne had asked her where he could find Brother Eli merchandise. At the time, she'd been helping a customer locate an obscure item on the microfiche and had broken the Maranatha customer service guidelines by simply pointing to the endcap near the back of the store. Shoot. Now she was upset with herself. The man had seemed out of place and rough around the edges, but she was always ready to believe the best about people. This wasn't the first time she'd been a bad judge of character.

She picked up the rest of the trash, a Hardees paper, another torn plastic wrapping and penny-saver ad sheet. Muttering to herself, she made her way to the registers and was formatting her incident report when the tinkling bell at the front door announced she had another customer.

Looking up, she saw a man shy of fifty, but with stark white hair blown back off his forehead accentuating his deeply tanned skin. His teeth too were brilliant, but he was not smiling when he asked where the Brother Eli display was. Gloria began to walk him to the back corner, but he stopped her and said, "Just point."

She smiled, blinked, and did so, then turned back to the register thanking heaven she'd just straightened the wrecked display. Behind the counter, she threw out the trash, but held on to the penny-saver thinking she would browse it before tossing it. Placing it beside the register, a manila envelope fell from between its pages onto the floor. She stooped to pick it up.

It was light and unsealed. When she looked inside she saw that it contained a photograph. She looked up to see if her customer was watching while she removed it. A detective's sense awakened in her and she believed she might be able to identify the shoplifter from the photograph. She smiled too as the idea to tape the photo onto her incident report followed naturally. She was on a roll.

She held the picture in her hand and turned it over, revealing what she first mistook for a bald man standing in front of another wearing a cheap wig. Then she gasped and felt her stomach clinch. She slapped the photograph face down on the counter when she noticed the tan man was standing in front of her.

Her face was white and she was too surprised to speak. Without a word the man placed his hand upon her own and slipped the picture into his palm. He held it up to his face for a moment before calmly slipping it into the breast pocket of his blazer. Then he looked deep into Gloria's face and held her gaze like a doe's. He shook his head back and forth subtly and placed his index finger lightly to his pursed lips before walking out of the shop.

Gloria couldn't get the image out of her head. The perspective was weird, the focus was slightly off, but there was no mistaking what was going on. No one was going to believe her if she wrote it down in the incident report. Especially if she said who the guy wearing the wig had looked like.

CHAPTER THIRTEEN

TERRY

They'd spent a hell of a confusing night in jail, thinking they'd been nabbed for the Mickey Mouse liquor store job. They were all clammed up until the fat ass deputy with the lethal B.O. and coffee breath had asked him what his dog's name had been.

Terry'd mumbled "What?"

The deputy said, "I had a dog before I got married. Big girl. Lab-Shepherd mix. But when she was about ten, my son was born and he had bad allergies to her, had some other respiratory problems, but y'know we could deal with the dog one, so she had to become an all-outdoor dog. She got hit by a car one night. Got out of the yard and wandering around the highway, just darted out in front of someone. Broke me up. What was the dog's name?"

"I don't know."

"Hickerson, what was your dog's name?"

Terry raised his head. "What? My dog? Layla?"

"How old was she?"

Terry sat up. "Wait. Hold on. What's my dog got to do

with anything?"

"Layla?"

"Yeah."

"She's dead, Terry."

"What?"

"She was in the truck."

"Oh shit. My truck was stolen." Terry had vaguely remembered it had been missing the day before or a hundred years ago. It felt like forever, but suddenly it started coming back.

Deputy Musil had seen a light in Terry's eyes for the first time since they'd brought him in. "Stolen?"

Terry was becoming more animated. "Yeah, it was missing yesterday. Do I need to file a report? My dog is dead?"

"She is."

It was Terry's turn to slap the table. "You catch the guy?"

It was Musil's turn to slump a bit. "Not exactly. There was an accident."

"And Layla's dead?" Musil had gotten up and headed for the door. Terry, suddenly interested in continuing, called after him, "Wait, tell me what happened."

At the door, Musil had paused. "There was an accident. Your truck was totaled and your dog was killed. So was the driver."

"Who was driving?"

The policeman had left the room at that point and an hour later both he and Cal were out and free. They'd traded covert looks of relief in the back of the cruiser they'd been given a lift in.

"Take us to Blaylock Drug. Need a drink."

"Let's just go to The Gulch then," Cal suggested.

"I'm not taking you to a bar," their driver put in.

"I don't wanna go to the fuckin Gulch, man. I just wanna get a case and kill it at home. Pass the fuck out."

"Okay," Cal had agreed. "Take us to –"

"We're not making any stops. I'm taking you home."

"Just drop us off at Blaylock, we'll walk the rest of the way."

That had been okay with the deputy, and at the drug store they'd purchased a case of Stag and marked their path home with discarded gold cans.

It took three hours to free Cal's truck from Terry's yard. The ground was soft from rain and they dug deep ruts spinning his tires in the slick grass. The difficulty of the work was also exaggerated by their general fatigue, as well as the celebration beers they ingested with the gusto of the recently-freed.

Things weren't all awesome though. Terry's truck was wrecked. If he'd had insurance on it, he'd be covered, but he didn't and he wasn't. Also, his dog was dead. There were always more dogs to get, but he missed Layla. The old bitch had been with him a long time.

And the sheriff's daughter.

Well that was too bad, but he never thought it was really going anywhere. And now he for sure had to look out for law enforcement. Sheriff was going to be on his ass.

Cal's eyes were black and his nose was grotesquely swollen from banging it against the steering wheel when they'd been arrested. Looked like he was wearing a bandit mask and his voice was all stuffy and whistle-y. He looked like a damn Muppet really. Terry stopped his work and looked at his partner's pale head peeking out between long, thin strands of red hair becoming heavy with sweat, his mouth continually open for breathing and he listened to the grunt and whistle of exertion. Cal was trying to lodge a tree branch beneath the back tires for traction. His already mangled features were further distorted by concentration. He was taking great puffing breaths through his open mouth and spitting every twenty seconds.

Terry just sat down on the lawn and began to chuckle. Cal looked at him and paused. "What's so funny?"

Terry began to double over.

"What?" demanded Cal.

Terry laughed harder.

"What the shit is so funny?"

Terry rolled onto his side.

"Think this funny? Think this–" Cal wrenched the tree branch free again and began to swing it at the back end of his truck, "–is funny?"

Terry began to hoot and Cal swung again at the truck, taking out a taillight. The pop tickled Terry further and Cal turned the branch on his hysterical friend.

He swiped furiously and repeatedly at Terry who rolled into a ball and covered his head. Cal rained down the punishment, concentrating on the back of his legs and shoulders. Terry's hysteria only increased and Cal's fury melted into a laughing fit of his own. He dropped the stick and fell to the lawn himself. "Oh shit."

"I thought we were so fucked."

"I thought you were. I was ready to flip on you."

Uncoiling gradually from his protective ball, Terry kicked Cal in the shin. "The fuck out."

"I was gonna tell em all about the photos of you getting tugged by a preacher queen in a queer shithouse." He laughed harder when Terry kicked him again. So Terry kicked him more. "I still can't believe you did that."

"Shut up," said Terry, his mood changing.

"Can't believe you could even get hard for it." His laughing reached new levels and he covered his face as Terry rolled on top of him and began punching. "Ow! Hey! Shit! I ain't judging you. Just, shit! Surprising, you know? Fuck!"

Terry caught Cal's forehead at an odd angle and sprained his wrist. Cal hooted and Terry gave up hitting him and caught the next wave of giggles instead.

They'd lain low since. Cal had impressed upon Terry the need to get a job for cover when their blackmail money came in. He had to have some reasonable source of income, Cal had said, which is why Terry was now catching a ride with his friend every morning to construction sites and getting a refresher course on the machinery.

Making money was a pain in the dick. He preferred to steal it.

Irm and Big Randy sat at opposite ends of the tweed couch in Darlin's office. There was a video playing in the VCR. Redneck vampire clan traveling around Oklahoma or somewhere in a Winnebago had stopped at a shitkicker bar and things were about to get bloody. Irm was lighting a joint and Randy cleaning a shotgun. She offered the big man a hit.

"Nah, thanks, Irm." Randy and most of the staff at both Chowder's and Darlin's had been on edge in the weeks since Dale whathisname had disappeared and Tate Dill had been let go. Chowder had stepped up security, keeping two people on every shift at the bait shop and hanging around Darlin's almost around the clock. He'd told Randy to clean all his guns and make sure they were handy which didn't exactly encourage relaxing in anybody. Except Irm.

Recently, Irm's demeanor had cleared considerably. She wasn't sulking anymore, in fact she was nearly as cheery as anybody could recall. Not that she whistled exactly, but she smiled once or twice and occasionally told a joke. She shut all the windows and closed the doors to Dutch-oven Randy earlier in the evening and the ghost of that nuclear fart still clung to the split ends of his bangs. He didn't know what to make of it, but had sense enough not to ask questions and to stay alert. Last thing he needed was for Chowder to walk in and catch him getting stoned on watch. His boss was as tense as Irm was loose.

The lethargic splat of water drops hitting the plastic shower curtain in the back room signaled the end of Chowder's nap and made the muscles in Randy's shoulders knot tighter. Irm sensed his tensing and insisted he take a hit, which he reluctantly and gratefully did. One would help. Irm watched him concentrate on it and a sly smile came over her face.

When Randy stopped holding his breath and exhaled a plume of smoke, he coughed three times before passing the joint back and sinking into the couch. He inhaled deeply through his nose and immediately began coughing and gagging again. "Oh, fuck!"

Irm rolled on the couch, cackling.

"Damn, Irm, what are you eating?"

"S.B.D."

"You need to see a doctor, seriously, you've gotta have the colon cancer." Irm laughed harder and took another hit. Randy thought he might prefer sulky Irm to this mirthful and flatulent version. He got up off the couch and stumbled for the kitchen and a glass of water. The air was fresher inside the refrigerator for once and he stuck his head in and breathed deeply while digging for a snack.

"Don't even think about touching my chili," said Irm from the other room, still chuckling and sighing with satisfaction.

Not a chance, thought Randy.

"Fuck's sake, Irma," Chowder growled.

Randy shut the fridge and got an empty glass he stuck under the tap for a drink.

"Open a window."

Randy turned around to see his boss entering the kitchen, shirtless and running a towel through his grey hair, dark with moisture. He put the towel to his face and vigorously dried his beard before draping the cloth around his neck.

"Randy," he acknowledged.

"Hey, Chowder." He averted his eyes to keep the outlaw from noticing any recently added redness. "You want a glass of water?"

"No."

"Okay. Is it alright if I have one?" Shit.

Chowder stopped and gave his full attention to the big man. He looked at Randy like he'd just shit the rug. "The fuck do I care?" Randy smiled, trying to make it look like a joke in retrospect. He turned sideways and edged by Chowder back out to the living room. He heard Chowder muttering to himself behind him and thought he'd volunteer to go make some rounds.

Chowder growled and Irm laughed. Randy exited the trailer grateful for fresh air and distance. He left the shotgun in the office.

Outside, sitting around the fire, three of the girls and six regulars were discussing the accident. Three weeks earlier, the sheriff's daughter Eileen had driven a truck right off the road and down a steep hill where she'd been caught and killed by a large tree. It was a big event for Spruce.

"I know that guy," said one of the girls.

"How's that? Which guy?"

"Customer. The one whose truck it was. Squirrelly."

"I would not want to be him right now."

"No kidding. Sheriff's gonna make it so he can shit from three holes."

Randy knew who they were talking about. Terry Hickerson had been a penny-ante douchebag till the sheriff's daughter had used his truck to go all Thelma and Louise with his dog and everything. Now he had a mortal enemy with a badge. Everybody was waiting for him to turn up dead, accidentally eviscerated with a can opener or hung by his nuts outside the elementary school. Or just disappear and never be heard from again.

Nobody would look into that too deeply.

CHAPTER FOURTEEN

CHOWDER

Chowder split the shades with his fingers and watched Randy talk to the folks outside around the fire. Irm was giggling in the next room. "Open a window, Irma. Smells like a retirement home in here." His shower had helped him clear his head, but already it was getting murky again.

He looked at his daughter on the couch, getting stoned and giggling at the TV. When he'd talked with her at the cabin, she seemed ready to sober up and take care of business. Take it seriously. He'd been feeling righteous about cutting his loose ends and just about ready to disappear. Take Hettie some place warm and let Spruce and the government kiss his ass.

Now that Mondale's daughter had been killed, the stability of everything was in question. Now was exactly the kind of time he needed a clear and cool head from Irm since he couldn't count on the sheriff. Listen to her.

"Hey," he barked. Irm quit laughing and sealed her lips around the joint. She lifted her eyes to squint at him, though.

"Sober up. I need you sharp." She nodded and held her breath. Chowder held out his hand, "Gimme that." Irm coughed out the smoke and gave her father the joint. Chowder ground it out between his fingers.

Irm didn't protest. She cleared her face of any trace of mirth. "I'm good. What's crawled up your ass?"

Chowder angled his body just right before letting himself fall onto the couch. He exhaled upon landing, then leaned his head back and pinched the top of his nose and rubbed his eyes with his fingertips. "This whole fucked up situation with the sheriff's girl. You heard anything from Tate?"

"No."

"What about Dale whatshisname?"

Irm nodded. "Nobody's gonna find that little shitstain."

"Okay. For now we just sit tight."

"I'm chilled out, Pop."

A low growl began to rumble out of Chowder as he tried to keep his voice conversational. "I know that Irma. I don't need you chilled. I need you sharp." He swallowed the growl and heaved himself upright. He walked to the back room to retrieve a shirt. When he came back into the front room, Irm still sat on the couch, but forward, elbows resting on her knees. She turned to look at him.

"I'm gone to see about the sheriff."

Irm nodded. "What should I do?"

"Lemme know if you hear anything."

"About what?"

"Anything." He opened the door, but paused with his back to her. "Just stay sharp."

Chowder stepped through and closed the door behind him, leaving Irm alone in the office. She waited a moment till she heard her father's truck pull out of the lot, then she rolled a new joint and put it between her lips. She lifted her hips off the couch to reach the lighter in her pocket and, once retrieved, set it against the stick in her mouth and sparked it. She took in the first hit, but started to smile and coughed it out prematurely. "Oops."

MONDALE

Mondale sat in his cruiser not listening to the radio or watching the traffic. He was off the road behind a sign that advised drivers to stay alert. The engine was cold and he was pointed at the spot Eileen had gone off the road. He'd been parking there every day after work for hours at a time.

His tunnel vision was zeroed in on the edge of the asphalt where the tire marks stopped. His little girl was dead, but all he could think about was how pissed Shirley must be with him.

He'd taken the chicken shit route and had Musil place the call to his ex-wife and she and her new husband had come to town immediately. Even his oldest daughter, only daughter, Liz had come down, seven and a half months pregnant, and between them they'd taken care of all the funeral arrangements. He had no idea how they'd even tracked down Eileen's friends. Handful of hippie, college kids from Kirksville she'd been closer to than anybody she'd grown up with. He was left now with the responsibility of caring for her grave and even that seemed like too much for him. If it had been up to him he'd have had Shirley take her body to St. Louis and bury her there. Now she anchored him here. She wasn't leaving. Neither was he.

The funeral had passed in a haze. Tears and condolences from the whole world. And food. So much food, but he'd barely eaten. His already wiry frame had tightened and become even more compact in the last few weeks. His uniform was too roomy and even his teeth seemed loose inside his skull.

He just wanted to disappear and get drunk. Nurse his hate. But he couldn't do that. Not with unfinished business. And not without drawing too much attention to it. For now he kept his drinking discreet. He did his job and stayed even-keeled. Everything he did was biding time. Waiting for the right opportunity, and gathering strength. Eventually the lethargy would slip away and he'd emerge from the cocoon reborn and consumed with a terminal rage.

And he would kill Terry Hickerson.

Back at the house, he'd climbed out of his clothes and into the shower. He'd sat under the scalding stream until the hot water ran out and then through the cold for another twenty minutes. He collapsed onto his bed without bothering to dry off and rolled onto his back. He closed his eyes and slept, but it wasn't rest.

He awoke early to someone at his door. He lay awake and listened to the persistent knock, not frantic, but not going away, until he broke and got up and slid into some pants. At the door was Bob Musil looking even worse than the mirror. He opened the door let his friend inside.

Musil looked him over approvingly. "Got some sleep. Good. How about some coffee?"

Jimmy just nodded his head and took a seat at his table while Musil went into the kitchen and set about preparing a pot for the two of them. He heard the tap running then stop and the sound of the machine being filled and turned on. Musil appeared in the doorway a moment later, leaning on his left shoulder against the wall. "Jim, I talked to Hickerson again."

Jimmy's guts constricted at hearing the name. "Jim, I just don't think he had anything to do with it." Jimmy just shook his head. "Seemed as surprised as anybody when I told him what'd happened."

"Bullshit."

"Said his truck was stolen."

The coiling inside him reached upward toward his throat, but he managed, "Why would she steal his truck?"

Bob didn't answer. He stepped back into the kitchen and began looking for clean mugs. Jimmy heard him opening and closing cabinet doors, then turning on the tap again. There was a hiss as Jimmy pictured Musil removing the pot from under the drip and then another as he'd be returning it. Bob reappeared with two mugs, steam rising out of both. He set one down in front of Jimmy and sat down with the other across from him. "I don't know that, Jim."

Mondale looked into his cup and saw his image reflected on the black surface of the liquid. He raised it to his mouth and scalded his tongue sipping it. Musil continued. "Didn't you say, she sometimes took your car when she came to town?"

"My car. *My* car, yes. Sometimes, but…"

Musil held his hands up. *Okay, I'll drop it.* "All I'm saying, Jim."

Musil waited for Jimmy to lift his eyes to meet his own. "Don't go and do anything stupid over Terry Hickerson. He's not worth it. Have you given any more consideration to taking some time off?"

Bob was spared being told to go fuck himself by a knock at the front door. Jimmy kept his back to it and stared violence at his deputy. Musil got up to answer. Behind him, Jimmy sensed Musil tensing up and the sound of the door opening. Heavy footsteps came into the house and Jimmy turned around to see his deputy standing in the front room with Chowder Thompson.

Musil said, "Call me, Jim." And left.

When the sound of deputy's prowler had died Mondale shrugged his shoulders, "What the hell, Chowder? You shouldn't be here."

Chowder ignored him and made his way toward the coffee pot.

"Any of the neighbors see you?"

Chowder came out of the kitchen and sat opposite Jimmy at the table with his own mug of black coffee. "Fuck you, Jimbo. You don't want me coming around? Answer your phone. You've kindly exhausted my patience."

"Aw," Mondale waved dismissively, "go fuck yourself."

"Gladly, once I know where we stand."

"What? What do you wanna know?"

"I need to know you're still ready to take care of business."

"Fuck you. I'm ready."

Chowder looked him in the eyes, "Yeah? What's going on with the ASA?"

"He's just rattling cages."

"And you know that how?"

Jimmy's voice was tight. "I've looked into it."

"It's my dick on the chopping block. I'm going to need more than that."

"Like what?"

"Have you reached out to him?"

"That would be a mistake. He's just a politician. He'll be distracted by something else soon enough."

"Don't have to remind you what you stand to lose." He waited for Jimmy to meet his eyes. "You are the straight face of a criminal enterprise. You run drugs and whores and do the occasional buy-off or murder to protect that enterprise. *They will string you up by your nuts with zeal.*" Chowder took a swallow of coffee. "And after that, will they come to see what service you performed for them and regret your crucifixion? No, they'll find some way of digging you up and doing it all over again."

Chowder took another drink while Jimmy looked at his.

"I can do prison, but I don't want to. I'd rather keep things as they are. We've got a situation or two deserving our attention and we need to have a serious talk. As a man with my own family, I sympathize. If you want the peckerwood chopped down, something can be arranged."

Chowder sipped the coffee and looked intently at his partner, watching for glimpses of his internal designs. Jimmy sipped at his own coffee and grimaced. It had gotten cold. Worse actually. It was getting cold. Cooling coffee was failing coffee.

The bitter taste of failure in his mouth, Jimmy lifted his gaze to the man before him. In Chowder's eyes was strength and clarity of purpose.

Jimmy said, "What have you got in mind?"

TERRY

Brother Eli's program was showing re-runs.

They'd mailed prints of the photos to him with a note scrolled in fat magic marker 'ELI ONLY' and, inside, another note saying they'd be in contact soon. They hadn't exactly worked out the details for collecting, but they figured they'd give him some time to think about it. Get worried. Terry was enjoying it.

The thought of Eli explaining his bruises to his wife and congregation and the board kept Terry whistling at work. He and Cal tuned in every night to see if Eli would appear on live TV or even a new taped segment, but they'd yet to see him. Cal would drive him home after work and they'd crack some beers, flip on the television and discuss how much money they should ask for.

"Ten million dollars."

"He'd never pay that."

"I know that. It's a negotiation."

"I don't wanna negotiate. I wanna get paid quick."

"We need to be reasonable. A lowish amount that he can afford to repeat later. If he's got a brain at all he'll know it's not a one time pay-off."

"Y'think?"

Cal ignored Terry's sarcastic tone. "Anybody dealing with the kind of money that TV station pulls in knows about those kinds of things. Any figure we throw at em will bounce around for approval."

"No way he'll tell anybody about it."

"We ask for too much money, he sure as hell will."

"Fuck. So how much you think?"

"I don't know. One million?"

"How 'bout two hunnert thousand?"

"I'm thinking more like thirty thousand with an annual repeat."

"No way. I did not do what I did for a lousy fuckin thirty

thousand. Fifty."

"That might be alright. He might be able to get his hands on that much."

"Well that's his problem, ain't it?"

Then they'd get high and the TV would get better. Eli's hairdo would begin to glow. When it came to life and reached out off the screen to fondle Terry, he changed the channel.

They decided to let Eli know they were serious. They sent a letter demanding ten thousand dollars be made ready for a drop off and that they would contact him with a location in two days. Eli was to wait for the location's identification in the food court of the Walmart on Branson Hills Parkway.

Two days later, Terry and Cal took turns browsing near the food court wearing disguises. They looked respectable with their hair combed back and their button down shirt sleeves and Terry even wore one of those cowboy ties decorated with a rhinestone. They pretended to shop for clothing, batteries and household wares while they waited for Eli to show.

After an hour of waiting Terry caught Cal's animated expression from across the room and followed his friend's subtle head jerks over to their mark. The preacher was wearing the same blonde wig and a pair of dark sunglasses, which Terry took for a sign that he was alone. No way he was going to wear that rug around his friends.

Terry walked away and headed for the phone bank at the south entrance. Cal had insisted that they look up the number for the manager's office instead of counting on there being a Yellow Pages there and it was a good thing because there weren't any directories available. He dialed the office and had them page "the gentleman who lost his photographs."

He had to wait three minutes before the preacher was on the other end of the line and Terry told him to leave the bag in the first stall of the men's room and then haul ass across town to the Marantha Family Bookstore where he'd find a personal photo.

The preacher's voice was harsh, but muted, "Fuck you and your penny-ante shakedown. Why don't I just keep my money?"

Terry was enjoying this more than he ever would the money. Having the important man jump through hoops. Having something on him and making him squirm. He let himself go silent and waited for the preacher to fill it.

"Hello?" Eli said. "Are you there? Answer my question. Why don't I just keep it?"

"I tell you what, Brother E. Go ahead and keep your money this time. Truth is, I already left that picture in that Christian book-store, right beside merchandise with your face printed all over it. You rush over there, you might get to it before anybody notices, so go ahead and keep it. Just know that if you do, I won't tell you where I'm leaving the next one."

CHOWDER

His eyes opened suddenly. He brought all of his senses out of sleep and into full alert and focus in less than a second. Hettie was asleep beside him and the clock said it was three in the morning. That was both early and late at different times in his experience. Either way it was fucked.

With an economy of motion he was out of bed, armed and at the back door. It was closed, locked and showing no sign of disturbance. At the front door, he turned on the porch light and peered through the curtain.

In the drive was a car he didn't recognize parked, waiting. The door opened and Tate Dill climbed out and leaned against the hood. He was alone. Chowder turned the light off and stepped onto the porch. "Looking to get yourself shot, Tate?"

"Need to talk to you."

"You only think you do. Get out of here. You come around again, you will get shot."

"Found Dale."

"Who?"

"Sloppy work, Chowder."

143

"I don't know what you're talking about."

"I know it wasn't you digging either. You know I'd never leave loose ends like that. I'm just saying, you need a number two with a competent streak."

"Yeah? Where'd you suggest I get one of those?"

"Hiring Dale was a dick move, I see that now and that's on me. But c'mon, bring me back, boss. You need me. And you need what I'm bringing to the table. I've got big plans, man."

Chowder shook his head. "I want you gone." He went back in the house and shut the door. He waited in the dark for Tate to leave. His ex-employee remained leaning against the hood of his car, looking right at Chowder through the window, though he couldn't possibly see inside in the dark.

When he spoke, it was in a quiet, conversational tone that meant that he knew he still had an audience and Chowder realized he'd been holding his breath.

"Forty-eight hours, Chowder. Think about it."

Then he got off the hood and back into his car. The ignition was silent and he waited till he was down the street to turn his headlights on.

Forty-eight hours. Little cunt. Chowder started the day's first pot of coffee.

CHAPTER FIFTEEN

MONDALE

Wanda Templeton had been a looker when it counted. She'd picked the cherry of half the graduating class of 1978, which didn't exactly endear her to the other girls her age, especially twenty years on as many of them had married those same boys. Wanda had stayed single and active after high school, but somewhere around thirty she'd started putting on weight and didn't stop. The heavier she grew, the more aware she seemed to be of the way she was regarded in the town. Years ago no one could've guessed she was so sensitive.

When his secretary opened Mondale's office door at nine o'clock she looked like she hadn't slept all night and she was angry to boot. Wanda threw a magazine on top of his desk and said. "Lies, Jimmy. They're all lies. I don't even know that man. I just wanted you to hear it from me first. I found that slipped into my locker this morning and I'm going to need to take a personal day. Maybe more." She burst into tears and ran out of the station before Jimmy could ask her to explain.

He watched her out the window get into her car and speed

away, then swallowed the bear claw he'd been ingesting when she barged in, washed it down with black coffee and licked his fingers clean before picking up the magazine. He'd finally begun putting a little weight back on. Since Eileen's death, he'd dropped ten pounds he could ill afford to lose. After his talk with Chowder, his priorities had begun to focus and purpose had given him an appetite again. Mostly he ate junk. But he ate. And he drank as much coffee as alcohol these days.

He looked down at the magazine that had so upset Wanda and picked it up. It was a smut rag opened to the letters department and accompanied by a photo essay of a muscle bound hayseed giving it to a big busted blonde wearing a cap with a badge on the front and holding an old standard issue six shooter. There was a particular letter that seemed to correlate to the photos and it was highlighted in yellow. The author's address was Hamilton County, Missouri and his last name was Hickerson.

The story wasn't about Wanda.

He fought the urge to run the lights and bleat the siren whenever someone pulled in front of him, but everyone on the road seemed to understand they best get the hell out of the way. When he'd finished reading the magazine, he'd rolled it up and stuffed it in his back pocket, checked that his weapon was loaded and walked out of the office. He'd felt the eyes of the whole world on him though no one would look at his face. In the parking lot they all seemed to be watching him, too.

He arrived at the Hickerson house under twenty minutes later. It took him a dozen strides to reach the front porch after he got out of the cruiser and thirty seconds of constant pounding for the door to be opened.

Thirteen-year-old Wendell opened it looking like the best parts of his daddy, which weren't many. He wore his hair shaved on the sides and long on top and flipped his head every few seconds to keep it out of his eyes, which were rimmed, red by beer or pot. He was a thin boy trying to look tough and mostly looking confused. His jeans were bunched around his unlaced army boots and the sleeves were cut off his flannel shirt, which was unbuttoned, and framing a black t-shirt that read Skinny Puppy, which was either a musical suggestion or monogram. The pathetic creature before him took some of the velocity off of the sheriff's heat-seeker.

"Your father here, kid?"

The boy pursed his lips and shook his head.

"You know where he's at?"

Again, Wendell gestured in the negative.

"Why aren't you in school today, son?"

Wendell shrugged.

Just then, from the back of the house, Terry Hickerson's voice croaked, "Who was that?"

Mondale looked hard into Wendell's eyes and the skinny puppy showed some pluck. He yelled, "Run dad, it's the police."

Mondale pushed past Wendell, who stared daggers at the big man. He could hear Terry Hickerson scrambling around the back and found the door partially blockaded. He put his shoulder to it and forced it open enough to see Terry's ratty-legged jeans shimmying out the window.

"Shit." Mondale ran back to the front door and around to the back yard sidestepping three decade's worth of junk, half sunk into the earth. He whacked his shin hard on a console television shell hidden behind a pile of plywood scrap and went down hard clutching his leg with both hands. He got back up and hobbled around the last corner and saw no sign of his quarry. "Shit whore."

Wendell was waiting for him back on the porch, looking defiant and scared simultaneously. He stood his ground though, which got to Jimmy a bit. "Tha〜 〜a〜 〜ute, son. Now where's he gonna go?"

Wendell backed up, but remained silent.

"Don't you think I'll come back looking for him? Don't you think whatever I've got in store for him is just gonna get worse?"

Wendell shrugged.

"That your answer for everything?"

Wendell started to shrug, but stopped short.

"Get in the car."

The kid's eyes swelled and he swallowed, but his feet didn't falter as he walked down the drive toward the cruiser.

Wendell stopped at the back door and placed his hands behind his back as if to submit to a cuffing.

"Up front. Get in."

Puzzled, Wendell did as he was told and Jimmy got behind the wheel.

"What grade are you in now?"

Wendell sat rigid in the passenger's seat and stared straight ahead. "Eighth. Where are we going?"

"Taking you to school."

In the time it had taken to arrive at school, Wendell's nerve hadn't faltered, but his outlaw's instincts were proving unformed and naive. Mondale's silent treatment was perplexing to him and maddening and five minutes into the trip, he began confessing to recent criminal activity.

Mondale let him keep talking.

"It was all me, too. My money, my pot." Wendell glanced nervously at the policeman who kept his eyes forward. "Yeah, I let my dad have some, but it isn't his."

"Give me a break, kid." He didn't have the stomach to listen to Terry Hickerson's son defend his father, King of the Douchebags. The poor kid knew a thing or two about the kind of man his father was, but still he was trying to shield Terry from the consequences of his actions. Dickhead would probably let him do it, too. Mondale wondered if Wendell knew that. Probably did. Kid wasn't stupid.

They pulled up in front of the school and Mondale had to go around to the passenger side and open the door before

Wendell would get out. He stood there waiting. "Get going." Wendell looked up at him and flipped his bangs out of his eyes for a better view. He was trying to read the policeman's intentions. "C'mon, I don't have all day."

"I'm not arrested?"

"Hell, no. Get your ass in there."

"What about my dad?"

Mondale slumped. "What do you want me to say? He's on my shitlist."

"For what?"

"I haven't got time for this, get." He gave Wendell a push toward the school. The Hickerson kid made the most of it, looking hard for any spectators and not giving any backward glances.

Mondale went back to the driver's side, but stopped when someone called his name. He looked up and saw Julie Sykes coming his direction from the front doors of the school. He hadn't seen her since the funeral, where he'd barely acknowledged her. He hadn't been returning her phone calls either. It was too fuckin weird, especially since Eileen's death.

"What's going on?" She was right beside him now. He could smell her.

"I've got to go, Julie." He opened the door.

She looked angry. "Why won't you return my calls?"

"I've just been busy." He started to get in.

"Bullshit."

She was right. He was full of it.

"I can't talk now." He closed the door and started the car.

Julie leaned on the open window. "I'm coming by tonight." She waited till he looked her in the eye. "Be there."

TERRY

It was his turn with the kid this week. Beth was out of town with some new boyfriend who was going to take her all manner of places she'd always whined about wanting to visit. *Good luck, bro*, thought Terry. *See if she lets you in the back door now.* Since Wendell was with him and he had to work hard to score points in the dad department, Terry'd decided to teach him how to score pot. He figured since he was eighty-sixed from Darlin's, it might be good to have the boy start running certain errands for him.

Wendell had been scared, Terry could tell. "Relax, it's not like on the TV with the guns and scary blacks and shit. Just try not to look like a pussy." He was thirteen and it was embarrassing how soft the boy was. That was his mother's fault. She was always spoiling him, always cuddling him as a baby when he cried. Maybe that shit worked with girls, but you had to be tough on boys. It's a cruel thing not to whip boys, they've gotta learn about things young so that they can handle it when the world takes off its belt.

So he'd taken Wendell around to see his new primary connect Enoch Tomlinson. Since the sheriff had put Earl Sutter in county lock up and he'd been uninvited to Darlin's, Terry'd adjusted and sought out Enoch for weed and kept him in mind for other, slightly more exotic procurements, but he didn't like it. Mostly, he just didn't like Enoch, whom he'd been to the fifth grade with and taken an instant dislike to on account of his vinegary smell. There were also rumors in the class that Enoch had been caught fondling his own younger male cousin the year before and Terry had opinions about that.

He'd given Wendell thirty dollars and the briefest of instructions, mostly designed to test the kid's mettle. "If he shows you a gun, don't budge on the price and if he asks if you're wearin a wire tell him to fuck himself." Wendell had swallowed, but didn't say a word, just nodded in consent. "Now if he tells you to take off your clothes to prove it, just don't let him touch you." Terry'd winked and smiled inwardly at the anger briefly coloring his son's cheeks.

Wendell'd come back to the car ten minutes after gaining entrance to Enoch Tomlinson's home and morosely sat in the passenger seat. Terry stared at his son silently before prompting him verbally. "Well?" Wendell had simply dropped an eighth of an ounce baggie into his father's lap and turned his face to the window. "How much you pay?"

Wendell dropped a wad of damp singles on top of the bag and Terry'd smiled. "Shit, he likes you." Terry stopped short of telling him he'd done good, not wanting to make the kid's head swell, but for the first time in a long time, he felt a twinge of fatherly interest in his progeny. "Didn't let him touch you now, did you?"

Wendell just looked out the window and Terry started the car.

A bonus to having the squirt around and knowing how to do things like that and drive a car too was that Terry could get stinko at The Gulch without chancing another DWI on the way home. He pinned a note to his own jacket instructing the bartender, who would find him passed out or incapacitated, to get the kid out of the pickup on the corner to help him out the door. He was feeling spendy lately thanks to the capitulation of Brother Eli. He'd even shared some of the grass with Wendell and he had no financial reservations about drinking.

Cal, generally finding Wendell to be a drag, had opted out of his company and Terry'd spent the evening thinking of what he might say to Brother Eli next time he told him where he'd left a photo. He was damn near ready to quit the construction job altogether. Hell with Cal's caution. He intended to go full-time with this blackmail shit. It was easy and even better, it was satisfying on a level that holding up convenience marts never could be. For the first time in his life he felt like he had a purpose and that he could take pride in the work he was doing.

Seeing that little fairy in the wig, just about bursting into tears running down the length of the Walmart, clutching the bag to his chest, had filled Terry with a strong warmth and sense of well-being. The money they found in the bag abandoned in the men's room hadn't come close to feeling as good as the shrieks of anger and fear he could only imagine were filling the preacher's car at that time. The more he thought about it, the more he drank.

It must have been a hell of a night because when the banging in his head woke him up he was on his own bed. His jeans were wet and cold about the crotch, but the bedding looked to have been spared the worst of it. Wendell must've been stronger than Terry'd given him credit for. Managing him drunk out of the truck, into the house and then into his bed couldn't've been easy.

The banging started up again and sent regret throbbing through his head. He heard someone talking in the other room followed by the creak of the front door. "Who was that?" he called to Wendell.

"Run, dad! It's the police!" came the immediate reply.

Like a hung over robot, Terry's legs shot out from under him and carried him toward the bedroom door. He tipped over his dresser to block the way, then slid the window open and jumped through, kicking his legs spasmodically, and landed upon his head in the lumpy lawn outside his bedroom. As soon as he hit the ground, he rolled into a crouch and sprinted through the back yard into the woods, over the creek and north toward St. Louis.

After five minutes of flat out running, which had slowed to a sloth's pace, he fell to his knees and puked a puddle of yellow liquid that would surely kill the grass. Then he rolled over and passed out.

It felt like someone was trying to jackhammer their way out from behind his eyeballs. When he got to his feet and began the long trek to civilization, he tried to remember why he'd slept in the woods. He'd heard Wendell say 'run' and 'police,' and instinct had carried him to that spot, but he might've overreacted.

When he found that he was on autopilot, heading for The Gulch, he smiled. *Good old autopilot.* He was there before the jackhammer guy seemed close to getting out and Terry tried to tickle him to passivity with the hair of the dog.

Cal Dotson came in after a half hour and called out when

he saw Terry. "Hoah, the man of the hour." He beamed like Terry'd just made him a grandfather as he crossed the dark void between them and sat on the adjoining stool. Cal clapped Terry hard on the shoulder and then smacked the bar with equal enthusiasm. "Bartender, do not accept a dime from my friend here. Everything he wants today is on me. In fact," Cal looked around and counted the patrons up to two and announced, "next round is on me."

The bartender grunted, but the drinks were poured and didn't have to wait long to be picked up. Cal smiled at each of his benefactees and ignored their sour expressions while he explained the reason they were celebrating.

"My friend here is a published author as of three days ago." Nobody cared, but Cal continued. "And like all great authors, he confronts the establishment in his time and lives in mortal danger of its wrath, all the while sowing seeds of immortality in the hearts and minds of all those who read his words." He drained his Bud and signaled for another before the empty glass was on the bar. "His ideas, once released, can never be called back or quieted. They sally forth and do not return void."

The bartender poured himself a drink too, and said. "The fuck you going on about?"

Cal made as if he were sizing up the bartender and the clientele, then placed his hand upon Terry's shoulder. "You look, to me, like gentlemen of the world and, as such, it may warm your hearts to hear that Terry here fucked the sheriff's daughter." Cal smiled at everyone in the room and indeed, there was a mumbled appreciation of this claim.

A knot in Terry's gut slipped just a little. "And," Cal continued, "he wrote it all down." Terry felt his balls tingle, as Cal's story was just now beginning to cut through the alcoholic fog that gripped his mind, "and then he published the story, every pornographic detail, in *High Society* magazine."

The bartender raised his eyebrows and his glass. Terry saluted.

Cal gestured toward the outside world. "Everybody's

talking about it. Blaylock's is sold out and they're disappearing from all the liquor stores within fifty-miles. You, my friend, my hero, must take precaution. Please finish your refreshments and then go underground. Follow the drinking gourd and trust no one."

Ah, thought Terry. *Now it makes sense.* He began to giggle uncontrollably. The thought of Mondale finding the published account of his wild kid's kinky habits in the hands of every deadbeat loser in town made him happy. Cal joined him and after an interval, even the bartender smiled and poured another round.

"Bitch killed my dog." Terry managed and all three of them laughed harder.

After a few minutes, the wisdom of Cal's advice also began to creep in. The police had already been to his house. They were probably looking for him now. Mondale was going to nail his ass. He needed to create some distance between himself and Johnny Law. Suddenly panicked, he turned to Cal.

"You got any cash for me?"

Cal shook his head. "But such as I have I give unto thee." He took a set of keys out of his pocket and placed them on the bar. "Take care of her, amigo, and bring her back soon, but go now. Be smart."

CHOWDER

He was arriving at the Bait 'N More with things on his mind. Behind the counter Irm was deep into a magazine. Judging from the crumpled plastic wrapper resting beside her it was a titty-rag. Irm looked like she was chuckling. Of course. What else would she be doing? He thought about Tate's advice. He did need somebody reliable.

He leaned over her shoulder to get a peek at the reading material. Irm paid him no mind. "Something good?" he asked.

"You're gonna have to put a leash on your pal the sheriff, dad."

"What're you talking about?"
"Read this."

CHAPTER SIXTEEN

TERRY

Terry slapped the keys off the bar and clapped his friend on the back. Cal was right. He hadn't thought this through that well. He really should take off for a spell. Wendell would be fine on his own for a few days. Probably have the time of his life. Maybe even ditch his virginity.

He faltered through the door and into the oppressive sunshine. He found Cal's pickup outside and stepped into the cab. He smiled at a stranger eyeing him from across the street. He was now the famous outlaw who'd defiled the sheriff's little girl. He was still woozy and waved drunkenly at his public, but decided to skip taking a bow.

Cal's truck was parked in the last spot in the lot. God, it was hot out and the asphalt radiated the sun's punishment up from below. He knew the air conditioner would not be working and considering how many beers he'd had in the last fifteen hours and his already sloppily sweaty condition, he was going to have to stop for a drink of water like pretty soon. The brightness of the astral punisher flipped the switch on his headache and the dude with the jackhammer behind his eyeballs started up again.

He opened the door and fumbled with the hand-crank as he rolled down the window, then he fell onto his right side to access the glove compartment. Please please please have some sunglasses, he prayed. There weren't any inside and Terry added them to the list of necessities along with water, and maybe ice cream that he needed to stop and pick up.

The engine started right up and he was shifting into reverse when he heard the hood smash. Startled, he looked up into the cold dead eyes of justice.

Sheriff Mondale's fist left a ham-sized dent in Cal's truck. Terry glanced around and saw that they, indeed, had an audience. The Gulch emptied as well as the grocery on the corner. The clerks had abandoned their posts and stood with their faces smashed against the glass storefront to watch him die. Traffic stopped going both directions and the whole thing played out at half speed.

Cal stood there, in the doorway, guiltily nursing his beer while his best friend was about to be slaughtered. The sheriff walked around the front of the truck while Terry sat still and dumb. When Mondale got to the door, Terry pushed the lock down. Mondale reached in the open window and pulled up on the mechanism. Terry slapped it back down and started rolling up the window. Mondale pulled the glass completely out and the it shattered on the pavement.

The sheriff didn't bother opening the door. He reached for Terry, who slapped ineffectually at the giant hands, and hauled his cracker ass through the window. Mondale's grasp swallowed up Terry and held him by both hands, then by both wrists.

He slid Terry's left hand under his right arm so that he could hold Terry's right hand in both of his own. Terry started wailing a hysterical, high-pitched scream. "Please, no. No, no, no, no. I didn't know, I swear." His fingers wriggled and writhed, but eventually were subdued. When his middle finger was secured, Terry tried and failed to take a deep breath before the break.

The *snap* stopped time.

The finger dangled backward like a wet noodle. The wind leaked out of him and he sucked pathetically for more, but didn't find any. He saw flashes of red and white, though his eyes were squeezed shut. His lower lip vibrated with his desperate breaths and no one, absolutely no one, came to his rescue.

The process was repeated with far less struggling on his left side.

MONDALE

He let the little puke slide to the ground in shock. Jesus, look at him, pissing himself in the parking lot. Mondale's hands and arms were trembling with adrenaline and he tried hard to appear in control in front of their audience.

An audience. What the hell was wrong with him?

He took two steps back from the specimen curled like a fetus on the asphalt and gestured at that dickweed he was always running around with. "Get him outta here."

Cal Dotson finished his beer and handed the glass to someone standing by. He slapped another bystander on the arm and together they grabbed Terry by the ankles and armpits, reasonably careful not to jostle his fingers, which dangled obscenely from his hands, which he held rigidly splayed in front of him, like a stick-figure cartoon done by a five year old. Terry's eyes were open, but not focused on anything and it wasn't until they laid him in the bed of the truck and, in doing so, bumped his right hand against the floor that Terry showed any sign of consciousness.

The silence that had hovered over the scene since the second snap was shattered by a hoarse yelp, equal parts fierce and pathetic.

Mondale's phone buzzed insistently in his pocket. He took it out and checked the number. He didn't recognize it. No name attached. Probably one of Chowder's disposables. He opened it. "Yeah?"

"Where are you at?"

"Town."

"Stay put, I'm coming to you."

Jimmy looked at the crowd around him. "No good. Meet me at the spot."

"Jimbo?"

"Yeah."

"Have you seen?"

"Yeah."

"Don't do anything stupid."

"Yeah. Okay."

CHOWDER

He hung up his burner and prayed to hell Jimmy hadn't already skinned the little fucker alive. Something in the sheriff's voice was telling him it was a distinct possibility. The story Irm had shown him was bad news and if what she'd indicated was true, news was spreading. He started up the truck. The engine roared to life, still warm.

Every time he felt like he'd gotten ahead of the train, some wrinkle popped up and threatened to derail the whole thing. Fuck this. He was going to take Hettie and leave. Irm was a big girl. She could take care of herself and damn well learn the natural consequences of her actions. He backed the truck out of its spot and shifted into drive, then turned the wheel toward the road.

Fuck Jimmy, too. If he couldn't keep his shit together, Chowder was through holding his hand. Fuck Spruce, fuck Hamilton County, fuck Tate, fuck Bug, fuck Memphis, fuck motherfucking Terry Hickerson. Chowder was the only thing keeping *that* little shitstain alive and he was through doing that, too. Fuck. He stood on the brakes for a car leisurely pulling into the lot as he was trying to exit. *Never mind this big-ass truck barreling toward you, asshole, just take your sweet time. You own the road.*

Chowder leaned on his horn, but it didn't have the desired effect. Instead the car stopped, half in, half out of the lot. The driver didn't look apologetic or even startled for that matter. Slick in a tie and shades. Young guy with good hair and a gym membership actually throwing his car into park and getting out.

Chowder rolled down his window and stuck his head out. "Move your ass-wagon, shitbird." Cocky fucker looked at him and smiled. Shiny teeth too. He put his hand on Chowder's truck, just reached out and touched the hood like it was a wild animal he was soothing. He came around the driver's side and leaned on Chowder's window.

"Move your car and get the fuck out of my face before you lose your own."

The smile again and this time he took off his glasses. He had blue eyes. Looked like a damn movie star. "Charles Thompson," he spoke in a slow, easy-going drawl he probably practiced. Nobody'd called Chowder "Charles" since he'd dropped out of the sixth grade. "I've been wanting to meet you." He held out his hand to be shook. Chowder just stared at it. "I've just heard so much about you and for a long time now I've wanted to ask you in person, did you really take that guy's eyeball out with a spoon? That's one of my favorite stories."

Chowder smiled at the Assistant State's Attorney. "You're gonna have to be more specific. Which fella are you talking about?"

The lawyer lowered his voice just like they do in the movies. "I'm watching you carefully, Charles. Pretty soon I'll have enough to put you away for the rest of your life, so enjoy what time you've got left." He stopped leaning on the door and did a gay little two-finger salute.

Good advice, thought Chowder. With his middle finger extended out the window, he put a dog-sized dent in the lawyer's fancy car peeling out of the lot. As he pulled into traffic, his cell phone rang.

He answered on the third chirp. "What."

"Uh, boss, thought you'd want to hear about the sheriff."
Big Randy told him the news.

CHAPTER SEVENTEEN

MONDALE

When Chowder finally showed up at their fishing spot, he'd had the chance to read the High Society story three more times. Forget that he'd just assaulted a citizen in front of a large crowd, he wanted to do it again. He wished he'd killed the little shit. He looked at the busty lady cop in the pictures, her fake tits standing off her torso like they were allergic to gravity, her shaved snatch glistening with oil, her teased hair and heavy make up making her look twice her age and cold.

She was supposed to be Eileen? It was obscene.

Chowder's pickup pulled up beside his cruiser and the outlaw jumped out like he had an electric prod up his butt. He looked at Jimmy like he wanted to hit him. "What did I fucking tell you?"

Jimmy jumped out of his cruiser. Never mind the hundred pounds Chowder had on him, if he wanted a fight, he could have one. He threw the rolled up magazine right at his partner. "I don't give a damn what you told me to do."

Chowder caught the magazine and threw it into the bushes. "They took him to the hospital Jimbo. The fucking hospital. And the whole town saw you do it. Are you trying to go to prison?"

"Aww." Jimmy waved off Chowder's concerns. Chowder stepped toward him and Jimmy closed the gap. When Chowder shoved him, Jimmy cracked his chin with a sharp uppercut. He'd stunned the big man as well as himself, but Chowder recovered quickly and instinctually punched Mondale square in the mouth. The big man was angry, but in control enough not to put too much behind it. Jimmy staggered back two steps then charged him.

Chowder simply absorbed him, swallowing his entire attack. Mondale didn't stop struggling until Chowder pulverized his kidney with a single blow. Jimmy's knees buckled, but Chowder held him up and gently lowered him to the ground, then sat down beside him.

Jimmy clutched his side and sat beside the larger man and sucked for air with as much dignity as he could muster. Chowder spoke to him in a patronizing tone. Again, like he was a little kid getting lectured by his father. "You've got to let it go for now. Too many eyes on you and me."

Chowder helped him to his feet and into his prowler and Jimmy saw something else in the big man's expression.

"Listen."

"I don't think so," Jimmy said, thanking god he'd left his keys in the ignition. He didn't think he could've reached into his pockets for them now.

"We got more talking to do."

"No, we don't." Jimmy started the car and pulled away.

He wandered the hills, avoiding town till the sun went down. When the light was gone, he pulled onto his street and killed the headlights. He slunk into his house and pulled all the curtains. The answering machine was full of dial-tone messages and there was blood in the bowl when he pissed. He grabbed a beer and an icepack and was headed for bed when there was a knock on his door.

When he threw it open, Julie Sykes jumped back. "I called. Somehow I thought you might ditch me." Mondale just stared. He couldn't think of anything to say. "Can I come in, Jimmy?"

TERRY

Everything hurt. He was helpless like a fuckin mental cripple. Both middle fingers, broken near off, were taped to the ring fingers. Everything was hard to do, eating, dressing, bathing, driving. Forget about work, he couldn't handle a riding lawn mower, let alone a CAT, which left him many idle hours. And that was even worse. He couldn't shuffle cards or tug his meat, and daytime TV was for housewives.

He called Beth, which was an accomplishment in itself, and asked if she wouldn't mind letting the kid stay with him more while he was incapacitated. She agreed right away, which made him feel worse. That meant she was probably still getting some from that new guy. There was no satisfaction in getting what he wanted if it didn't involve depriving someone else of theirs. But Wendell would be helpful to have around. He'd do just about anything Terry asked, then retreat to a corner to remain unnoticed until needed again. If only his mom had been that way.

Thursday night, Cal picked him up at six and Terry told Wendell not to expect him back all weekend. His son took the news stoically and Terry wondered if the kid's delicate feelings were hurt or if he was stoked to have the place to himself. Sadly, it was probably the former. He was a strange kid. When Terry was that age, he'd have given his left nut for run of the house for a weekend. Oh well.

Cal was happy. Thursday was usually the best part of the weekend, and he regularly called out sick or just didn't go in to work on Fridays. "Our ship's come in, kemosabe."

"Say how?" said Terry.

"I sent the preacher more instructions."

"When the fuck did you plan on telling me?"

"Hmm. Right the fuck now, I guess. Chill. I only just did it last night."

"How?"

"I called him on the phone just like before."

"Hey genius, you know they can trace that shit."

"Only if they went to the police. You really think they're gonna do that?"

Terry thought no such thing. "Well, what'd you say?"

Cal smiled. "I was so fuckin smooth, man."

"Yeah?"

"Oh yeah. Told him to leave the cash in a bag inside a parked car at the Walmart in Sykeston."

"And where'd you put the picture?"

Cal started rocking back and forth with mirth, "In the baby station of the men's room at the roll-toss place." Terry too laughed at the idea of Eli going into the down-home-cookin, family-vibe restaurant to retrieve homo jackoff photos.

"So, you picked up the cash already?"

"Course."

"Well, where is it, dude?"

"At the house. It's in Aunt Jeanette's diaper bag."

"The fuck outta here."

"Pretty secure if you ask me."

"Alright then, shit, let's get wasted."

They headed for The Gulch and hit happy hour in the face. Each of them ordered a pitcher of Bud and three shots of Tequila. Terry shared his painkillers and the weekend had begun.

Two hours later the cocktail of motor skill assassins had rendered Terry clumsy and he spilled the last of his second pitcher and cussed. "At this rate, I'll be dry by Sunday."

"Won't let it happen, kemosabe," Cal laughed. He grabbed his own pitcher and took it over to the next table. Heck and Toby, two roughnecks already sitting there, weren't happy to see him.

"Fuck off." The older one said as soon as Cal had settled

and begun to pour himself another drink. Cal ignored him and drained half the glass in a single gulp. "Hey. Did you hear me? Fuck off, like now."

"Get bent, Heck."

"What did you say?"

"Go out back and play with each other quietly, so the rest of us can finish a drink," said Cal. Toby, the younger one, stood up and Cal kicked his knee from under the table with a steel toe. The young man fell and smacked his face on the edge of the table, sending all the drinks and glass that rested atop crashing to the floor. "Son of a bitch!" cried Cal, seeing his unfinished pitcher go to waste. He reached across the table and smashed his mug on the side of Heck's head.

Quickly as he could, Terry made his way over and began kicking Toby in the ribs. If Toby managed to get to his feet, Terry would be useless with his mangled hands, but it didn't happen. Terry connected the heel of his cowboy boot to Toby's temple and the youngster stopped moving.

Just then, a horse kicked Terry in the kidneys and he collapsed with a whimper. The bartender stood over him with a well-used baseball bat.

"Get the fuck out, now!"

Cal and Heck stopped their rasslin and together dragged Toby's unconscious body out the back door while Terry followed, unable to contribute because of his hands.

When they'd propped Toby up against some garbage bags, Terry made his contribution by taking out the last of his painkillers which all three of them split. Heck dry swallowed his then looked down at the man on the ground.

"Shit. There goes my ride."

"You can ride with us," said Cal.

"You are a white man," said Heck. "And I know a place."

"Oh yeah? Like a reasonable place? How much?"

Heck reached into his back pocket and took out his Saturday Night Special. "We can make a stop first."

Cal met Terry's questioning stare. They had money waiting back at Cal's place and didn't need to pull some chicken-shit stick-up for cash. But this wasn't really about cash, was it?

"Okey-doke."

MONDALE

Four A.M. and he'd slept perhaps three hours in short, fitful bouts, roused continuously by rage and guilt and lust. He slipped out of bed and dressed in the bathroom, pausing only to scrub his face with cold water. He was careful not to make noise and avoided even turning on the light, but when he opened the door Julie Sykes was sitting up in bed waiting for him.

"What's wrong?" she asked, to which a thousand answers immediately sprang to mind.

But he said, "Nothing. Go back to bed."

"Where are you going?"

He stooped to pick up his shoes and then headed out the door. "Work."

When he got into the car, he realized he'd been holding his breath. As he wheeled out of the drive and down the street he recapped the previous twenty-four hours. He'd read a pornographic story about his own dead daughter, assaulted the author in front of a crowd of onlookers, been in a fight with Chowder Thompson and fucked his dead daughter's high school friend. Jimmy Mondale, this is your life.

Julie Sykes was up for it. When he'd opened the door for her, she'd come in and tried to engage him in conversation about the day's events, but his non-inclination toward talk was obvious and when he'd reached for her like some automaton set on "fuck" she'd gone along without missing a beat.

And it was kinda weird.

There'd been no talk. Their coupling felt choreographed and unremarkable. Not bad exactly, but he'd participated in more exciting handshakes.

Afterward he'd collapsed on his back and gone straight to sleep.

When he walked into the station, Deputy Townsend

looked up from his magazine and then at his watch. "Hey, Jimmy." The young policeman glanced around, clearly uncomfortable in his presence. "What's going on?"

Jimmy ignored Townsend and closed his office door behind him. Ten minutes later he was asleep at his desk. Bob Musil woke him up around six. He stood over Jimmy with a cup of coffee and handed it over as soon as the sheriff could hold it. As Mondale took his first sips, Musil told him how it was.

"Take some time off, Jimmy. Not a suggestion this time."

Jimmy didn't have the energy to argue. When he got back home, Julie was gone and there a message on his machine from his ex-wife. Shirley's voice started talking directly to him, for once, mistaken, that he'd been standing there listening. "Jim, Elizabeth's gone into labor. We'll be at the Holiday Inn if you need to reach us. I'll call again soon with more news. And Jim? Pick up the phone next time."

He went to his bedroom and grabbed a pair of jeans and a t-shirt. He was fifty miles outside of Kansas City before he realized he had no idea what hospital to head to.

CHOWDER

Forty-eight hours were up with no word from, and no sign of, Tate Dill. He'd had Hettie begin packing for a clandestine exit. The cloak and dagger element excited her. They'd had a bout of aggressive two-minute sex after he'd told her to keep it quiet, then he'd gone into the Bait 'N More where he was working the four-to-midnight shift. He was reading travel magazines about destinations south when the movie star lawyer came through the front door. Chowder looked up and the lawyer waved at him as he headed for the salty snacks. Chowder's stomach acted like he'd eaten a fistful of nails while he watched the lawyer shop. A few minutes later he strolled up to the counter with bags of chips, cans of nuts, a large coffee and two-liter Vess cola. Then he stood in front of Chowder and leafed through the magazines. "You have *High Society*?"

"Sold out."

"Damn. Everybody is. Guess I'll have to find it elsewhere." He winked at Chowder and indicated that he was finished shopping and was ready to check out.

Chowder rang everything up slowly, mentally tracking the caloric value of the lawyer's purchase.

Dennis Jordan read his mind and laughed. "I know, disgusting isn't it? I don't usually eat like this, but y'know, stakeout food."

Chowder nodded. "You're gonna have to leave the parking lot. Got a no-loitering policy."

"Spotted me, huh? There's a ding in the back of the car I oughtta fix. Be more discreet."

"What are you hoping to see happen?"

Jordan shrugged. "My primary target left town this morning, so I'm just observing another one now. Probably nothing'll happen tonight, but you never can be certain."

"I see. Who's your primary target?"

"Sheriff Mondale."

"Oh."

"Yeah, he split pretty quick. Packed light and left town. I lost him, I'm embarrassed to say. You have any idea where he might've gone?" Chowder shrugged. "Well, if you have any ideas, lemme know, huh?"

"Why would you want to follow Jimmy Mondale?"

Jordan put his hand on top of a bag of chips and his voice became mock sincere. "No offense, Charles, but you're just not the bigger fish here. When I take down Jim Mondale it's going to make my career." He stifled a grin and added, "I'm sorry, you didn't think I was really spending all this energy coming after you, did you?" He broke out that movie-star smile and amped up the wattage. "Now that's cute." He let the smile slack a little. "You've made a good name for yourself, Charles. Really. Good for you. You wanna keep that good name, though? Help me help yourself and your family. Mondale's lost it. He's going down and who knows what he'll do to keep that from happening?"

Chowder's stomach bubbled audibly.

"Just saying, those who come to me first, before accusations start flying? Usually get the better shake." He picked up his groceries and popped a handful of chips into his mouth and munched them noisily. He started to leave, but stopped and turned to Chowder. "Speaking of accusations flying. Any truth to the rumor it was your daughter who ran the sheriff's little girl off the road that night?" He studied Chowder's face for a moment. "No? Hmm. That's good. I'd hate to see something bad happen to her when the sheriff gets wind of the same rumor. I hope people quit saying that. She sure seems like a real sweet girl."

He walked out the front door and toward his car parked on the far side of the lot where it'd been for an hour. Chowder wiped the counter free of crumbs from the chips and found Assistant State Attorney Dennis Jordan's card left there for him. He picked it up and held it close to his face to study.

He started to throw it away, but stopped. Then he put it in his wallet.

CHAPTER EIGHTEEN

TERRY

The Mexican population was a small, but growing minority in Hamilton County, a fact that alarmed most of its citizens. They were a cluster that were rarely spotted outside the borders of Beantown, but were large enough to have their own grocery store in Spruce that stocked mini tortillas and a rainbow coalition of salsa and beans. They also had their own video store with Mex titles starring big-tittied, big-hipped Mex starlets. The movies were big on guns and mustache wax. They also had their own liquor store.

The volume wouldn't be large enough to make a worthwhile score of the cash register, but there was a neighborhood Mex lottery held on Friday nights and Heck figured they could hit that stash tonight for enough to make a good weekend for the three of them at a brothel he knew in West Memphis.

One advantage, Heck figured, was that it probably wouldn't even be reported to the police, seeing as how the lottery was unregulated. "Rock on," agreed Cal as Terry opened the window so that the breeze would brace him enough to be a getaway driver.

They parked across the street and Cal put the car in neutral and pulled the parking brake. Terry slid beneath the wheel and rested one palm on top and one on the stick. "I got this bitch," he said, confident on adrenaline and racial superiority.

Cal popped the glove box and grabbed a mask, then he and Heck strode across the pavement like it was the streets of Laredo. Heck kicked open the door unnecessarily and the cowboys charged in brandishing weapons. With the windows rolled down, Terry could hear the muffled shouts and make out the flailing of arms between the window posters for exotic Mex liquors and Budweiser, the king in any language. He wished that he were in there too. The testosterone surge had produced instant facial stubble and he thought about what kind of whore he'd select for the weekend.

It was taking longer than usual for one of these jobs, but he figured that was to be expected since there would be a separate safe for the lottery money. Maybe the greasers were giving them trouble about it, denying it and playing dumb.

Fucking beaner trash, he thought. *Give it up.*

A small contingent of civilians was beginning to collect on the sidewalk, somehow aware that something was going down. Spooky how the ethnics were connected like that. A couple of them even turned and looked at Terry who extended his bandaged middle finger to them out the window. He revved the motor as the front door burst open and a masked Heck emerged pistol in one hand, grocery bag in the other. The glass door shut behind him and was instantly painted red in a single blast.

Heck didn't even turn around. He sprinted across the street and began fumbling with the door handle. Terry stared at the shop door as the red paint began to slide down, effluvia separating and streaking the now-cracked, spider-webbed glass. It was flung open again and a stout Mexican woman with a shotgun stepped over the headless corpse of Cal and took aim at the car.

"Go, go, go." urged Heck.

"Shit, shit, shit." countered Terry. The car lurched and died at the same moment Heck was flung across the seat and into Terry's lap. He was missing the right side of his face. "Shit, motherfuck!" The car started again and Terry pushed Heck to the other side of the cab. He clipped a parked car and had to use the back of his right hand to clear the blood and hair from the windshield. He succeeded only in smearing it before he had to shift again.

The car lurched a second time, but didn't die, and he picked up speed while the back window exploded. A sharp pain in his neck turned warm instantly and he gunned the car. Reaching to the windshield again, he scrubbed harder and cleared a window just large enough that he was able to register the streetlight before he struck it.

MONDALE

He found the hospital by calling each one on the list he got from information, asking for Elizabeth's room number till he got a hit. He trolled the gift shop for an appropriate card to express himself and settled on a tasteful black and white image of a woman with a newborn baby cradled against her. Inside, the sentiment was rhymy and he didn't quite follow it, but figured that wasn't too important. He had to borrow a pen to sign it with and then froze up deciding what to sign. "Dad?" "Your Father?" "Love?" "Sincerely?" "Jimmy?" He ended up scrawling "I love you," and left it at that. Then he folded the card gently into his breast pocket.

He had no intention of barging in there uninvited, but made himself comfortable in the waiting room and settled in for the night.

Shirley found him a little past midnight, on her way to find some food. "Jimmy, what are you doing here?"

Mondale smiled at his ex-wife and the reality of the situation broke through to him for the first time. He reached out to hug her without thinking. "Hey, Grandma, how's our girl?" He kissed her neck and took a deep sample of her smell.

"Liz is great, Jim, and Lilly is beautiful. You should go in and see them."

"Not yet. I don't want to intrude. I know nobody is expecting me tonight."

"You're right, there. But it's great you could make it. Liz may give some attitude, but she'll be happy to see you."

"Where are you going?"

"I'm on a mission. We're starving."

"Can I come with you?"

Shirley hesitated only a second. "Of course. Come on, Grandpa."

They took Shirley's car to the twenty-four hour Dunkin' Donuts where they loaded up on pastries and coffee. Jimmy insisted on paying and listened to her recount the story of the labor and delivery. The two of them should be proud, she'd said when they got back in her car, their little girl had done so well. Neither spoke for a moment and Shirley didn't start the car. Jimmy looked at her and saw the tremble in her lips. It triggered his own and they both began to cry simultaneously.

Jimmy reached for her and she allowed him to hold her, sliding her arms under his and around his back. She snorted and Jimmy squeezed her tighter. "I'm so sorry, Shirl, I'm so sorry. It's my fault, it's –"

"No, no, it's not, Jim. She was –"

"God, I miss her so much." She gripped him so tightly he didn't think he'd be able to breathe. He cried harder than he had since childhood and completely lost control of it. There was no reigning it in now. Great heaving sobs racked him and he buried his face in her shoulder.

For ten minutes they clutched each other and Jimmy never let up. After some time, Shirley took his head and laid it in her lap and stroked his hair. He let her do it while he continued to shake. "Shhh." She soothed him until he was finished.

"I'm sorry I was no use at the funeral."

"Shhhh."

"I fell apart, Shirl."

"We've got a beautiful granddaughter waiting for us to spoil her." He picked himself up and wiped his nose on his sleeve. Shirley reached into the Dunkin' Donuts bag for napkins, which she used on her shirt and jeans.

His phone began to vibrate in his pocket and Jimmy fished it out. He checked the number. Chowder's disposable again. He ignored it. "Oh, man, Shirl. I'll buy you some new clothes."

Shirley began to chuckle. "I am a mess."

TERRY

He woke up in a hospital room. Nurses came in every half hour, police too, but he wasn't speaking yet. He barely registered anyone's presence. Someone snapped their fingers and he followed the sound to a deputy who spoke his name.

"Hickerson. Terry Hickerson. You hear me?"

He must have nodded his head because the next thing he knew they were wheeling him out of the hospital and taking him to the police station. At the station Terry was seated at a folding table in the break room that doubled for an interrogation space. His head cleared disturbingly quickly as he eyed the Doritos in the vending machine and his stomach bubbled. The deputy came back in the room ten minutes later with two Styrofoam cups of weak government coffee. In the light, Terry read his name: *Musil.*

"What the fuck time is it, Deputy Musil?"

"Two-thirty."

"What time you feature I might get to bed?"

"Just depends on your willingness to cooperate."

"Shit, then I am never going to sleep tonight."

"I just want you to answer a few questions."

"See, and I don't want to."

Musil took a sip of coffee and swished it around his mouth. He smiled a sad smile at Terry like he pitied him. It pissed Terry off. Musil leaned back and turned his attention toward the snack machine. He said, "These damn apple pies are making me fat. See, the problem is that coffee is a necessity and what's available here is shit." Musil indicated the coffee in front of Terry, which did look poor. "The only thing that makes it drinkable are these sugar bomb 'pastries' and the only thing that makes them tolerable is the bitter-ass coffee."

Musil punched a button and the machine shat out a green paper-wrapped apple pie. The policeman peeled it lengthwise, like a banana, and tore off a corner causing white cracks to shoot through the sugar coating. "I bet I could leave one of these in a bowl of milk overnight and it wouldn't be soggy in the morning." He popped the piece into his mouth, took another swig of the coffee and swallowed. "Terry," he said, "this has got to be your shit year."

Terry had no objections to that statement, but he had some designs on turning it around. "I know, y'all are about as tired of my ass as I am of yours, so how 'bout you just lemme get on home and go to sleep."

Musil chuckled. "You're half-right. But you're gonna have to do a lot better than saying 'please' to make me let you go home."

"I know how this works, so how bout this: how 'bout I give Chowder Thompson to you on a plate?" He let his offer hang in the air and settle over the fat cop. It looked to be having the desired effect. He had the policeman's full attention. "He's a drug-running pimp parked in your very own back yard, and I will bring him in. Would that interest you? Why don't you go ahead and get me a lawyer while you consider what that'd be worth to you?"

CHAPTER NINETEEN

CHOWDER

Irm was on the couch in Darlin's office, half-baked and watching TV when Chowder arrived. Randy peeked his head in from the kitchen and Chowder told him to get lost. Randy grabbed his breakfast and took it outside while Chowder looked at Irm watching *Ren & Stimpy*.

As soon as he was out the door, Chowder walked over to the television and snapped it off. He turned to Irm who looked up at him, impishly amused by his frustration. After a moment, she said, "Yes?"

"You heard any interesting rumors lately?"

She shrugged.

"About yourself?"

Irm straightened and shook her head. "Like what?"

"I'm hearing that you ran Eileen Mondale off the road." The control he had on his voice was slipping. Irm was stonewalling him. "Killed her."

Irm looked him in the eyes for ten seconds then tried, "Sorry?"

177

Chowder turned around and kicked the TV off its stand, but when it failed to shatter on the rug he put his fist through the kitchenette wall. "Tell me it's not true."

"It's not true?"

Chowder's face turned purple and Irm chuckled.

"Was an accident. She was driving that asshole's truck. I was just trying to fuck with him. Who the hell is saying this anyway?"

"Assistant State's Attorney. Wants me to help him bring down Mondale."

Irm looked interested now. Invested. She sat up. "Well, I hate the sheriff, but fuck that."

"Yeah, well it's all of it fucked now, Irma. If I don't turn on the sheriff, he's going to tell Mondale what you did."

"Can't prove anything."

"He doesn't have to, Irm."

Irm nodded her head and smiled.

"You want to go to prison?"

"I'm not afraid of prison."

"The choice between going there and not is no choice at all."

Irm rolled her eyes. "Spare me, dad. He's your friend and your problem. You want my help, just ask."

Chowder picked up the cheap metal chair in front of the desk and hurled it across the room. It put marks in the plaster of the wall on the far side.

Irm stood and bumped him with her chest. "I am ready to help you, old man, but I am not prepared to take any more of your shit." She poked his sternum with two stiff fingers. "You've been playing house with the police so long now, you think it's what you want." She turned and walked toward the kitchen. "I suppose it's got advantages, but I'm prepared to live the other way. Just cause you got old and comfortable don't mean the world did too." She opened the fridge and grabbed a beer in a can. Popping the tab, she continued. "So just say it, dad. Who do you want me to get? You want me to pop this lawyer? Want me to make sure the sheriff don't ever hear about it? Say it."

Chowder pointed at her. "Just stay out of my way."

He slammed the door as he left.

MONDALE

Holding his granddaughter had sobered him up. Priorities reasserted themselves and all the world's problems were reduced into neat stacks he organized instinctually into two camps: things I give a shit about, and all the rest. He looked around the hospital room at his daughter lying there all swollen and exhausted, but glowing and proud, her dull husband oozing protectiveness and parental instinct, his ex-wife watching him hold the future in his arms and not a drop of ill will or condescension in her stance, and Jimmy couldn't deny that even her new husband, the man who made a cuckold of him, belonged here. He realized that everything outside the door belonged in the latter category.

Lilly's eyes opened halfway and he held her face near his own. They smelled each other. She moved her mouth, opened and closed it twice and that was all. She closed her eyes again and he kissed her and handed her over to proud papa. Then he knelt over Elizabeth lying in her recovery bed and whispered. "So proud of you, sweetheart."

"I love you, Dad," she answered.

He replayed the scene non-stop on the drive home. He had elected to leave while he was ahead. Give everybody some space and not push his luck.

He pulled out his phone to hear his messages. His mailbox was full. Everybody thought they had important things to tell him, but they were wrong. Chowder had left three messages of escalating urgency. Bob Musil said that they needed to talk right away, and Julie Sykes was demanding he return her call. He thought he'd start there.

She picked up on the second ring. "Hello."

"Hey, I thought you might be working."

"Jimmy? Yeah, I'm on my lunch break."

"Good. Listen, lemme take you to dinner tonight. I've been a jerk and I want to make it up to you."

She chuckled, a little unsure of herself. "Yeah, you've been a pill."

"Look, Lizzy had her baby last night and I'm on my way back from Kansas City right now."

"Oh my god, Jimmy, you're a grandpa."

"You still want to have dinner with me?"

"Yeah, of course. We'll celebrate."

"Alright, I'll call you when I'm back."

They agreed to talk later and Jimmy crossed one item off of his to-do list. On to the next. He got Musil's voicemail. His deputy must have been working the late shift last night and been asleep at the moment. "Bob, it's Jimmy. I've been in K.C. Liz had her baby last night. Lilly Eileen." He choked on the name, but caught himself and recovered quickly. "She's seven pounds, six ounces, twenty-one inches, and perfect. Give me a call when you're up. I'll be back soon." He started to hang up, but added, "And Bob, listen, I'm uh, I'm good. I'm better now. Don't have to worry about me. Thanks."

He punched in Chowder's number and turned the radio up as Otis Redding's "These Arms of Mine" began. He was humming along when Chowder's gruff voice cut through. "Called you fifteen hours ago."

"What's going on?"

"We have to talk."

"On my way. Hour and a half wherever you want." They made arrangements and hung up. Jimmy rolled his eyes. Touchy.

TERRY

He woke up in his cell feeling thick. A pain behind his right eye was his compass, but he was unable to make satisfactory sense of his surroundings. He tried to sit up, but was unable to correctly gauge his vertical and over-rotated, catching himself on his elbow lying on the other side. The weight of his head was like a bag of bowling balls and he dipped forward. He snapped his head up and used his hands to help steady himself.

The light inside was oppressive and he squinted to minimize it. "Hello?" he croaked, barely audibly. There was a scraping sound on the floor as the policeman sitting outside his cell moved his chair.

"Hey, you're alive."

"Water?" Terry said, as if he were unsure such a thing existed.

"Sure thing, buddy. You're in luck, there's a drinking fountain in your cell, there. Go ahead, help yourself."

If his thirst were not so severe, he wouldn't even dignify the policeman's sarcasm with a glance, but the suggestion of a cold drink was too much to resist. Of course there was no drinking fountain in the cell. The policeman had been referring to the toilet, which, in his present state, did look appealing. Really, it was pretty clean and he was sure the water would be cold.

Fuck it.

He bent over the bowl and heard the policeman chuckle. He cupped his hands and reached into the cool water and splashed his face. It did feel good. The next dip, he came up with a handful that he turned and splashed on the man in the chair.

"Shit!" cried the deputy.

Terry laughed. "I want my phone call."

"Good fuckin luck, shitbird." The policeman wiped water off of his face and got up to leave the room.

"Hey, I want a phone call and a lawyer." But Terry was already alone again.

MONDALE

He was pulling off of the main road onto the dirt path winding into the woods when Bob Musil returned his call. Jimmy picked it up. "Bob."

"Jim, where you at?"

"Almost home. What's up?"

Mondale could hear his deputy cupping his hand over the mouthpiece for privacy. "We've got a problem. Hickerson and two of his buddies robbed a liquor store halfway to Neosho last night. Cal Dotson and Heck Moeller were killed by the owner."

Shit. "What about Hickerson?"

"He crashed his car, suffered a concussion, but he's alright. We've got him in custody."

"What's the problem, then?"

"He's not keen on doing any time."

"No?"

"He's offering us Chowder Thompson."

Shitwhore.

"Says he knows all about Chowder's drug business and prostitution."

Mondale parked his car and shut off the engine.

"Jim, you there?"

"How long before you kick him loose?"

"Dunno. He's squawking for a lawyer. We've got him isolated. I gotta go now, so meet me at the Come Back Again in an hour, we'll hash it out, but we can't keep a lid on him much longer."

Mondale folded the phone back into his pocket and opened the door. He looked around him realizing that this land was once the wild west. And that it still was.

He said aloud, "The hell we can't."

CHOWDER

The place was a grassy, shady fishing spot outside of Spruce on the northeast edge of Hamilton County. It required a ten-minute hike to reach and that was the main reason they'd used it as a meeting place for so long. The remoteness discouraged spying. Here they could speak frankly and not worry about being seen together.

Chowder had his knife out, methodically stripping a tree branch when Jimmy Mondale appeared. Chowder dropped the smoothed stick and stood. "You picked a hell of a time to go AWOL."

"Keep your pants on, I'm here now and ready to work."

"Put your house in order, then. ASA is coming for you."

"Pencil-dick politician. He got anything?"

"Just a whiff, far as I know. But sooner or later he's gonna approach the right person."

"Who is there outside your family and my deputy?"

"I'm just saying."

"Fine. Meantime, that dipshit with the mangled hands is offering you to the government to keep his ass outta jail."

Chowder looked down and realized that the decision had been made long ago. "He's gotta go. Too bad the whole world saw you wreck his beat-off mitts the other day."

"Much as I'd like to do it myself," He looked imploringly at Chowder, then added, "we're gonna need witnesses to say I was elsewhere."

Motherwhoring shit-ass week.

CHAPTER TWENTY

TERRY

His head was clearing, unfortunately. As the painkillers wore off, the more sober he grew, the more he regretted it. Cal was dead. Shit, that sucked. Layla was gone, his truck was totaled, his fingers were useless and there was a powerful itch between his shoulders he couldn't reach.

The sorrier he felt for himself the stronger he grew. When he got out of here, he was going to fuck some shit up. He was going to burn down the world. He'd been bluffing with that whole Chowder Thompson thing. Just wanted to get out so he could split. He'd visit Cal's aunt Jeanette and get the cash out of her diaper bag then maybe he'd grab Wendell and they'd hit the road, hold up gas stations all the way to Mexico. Put some hair on the kid's nuts. He'd turn out alright after all.

What the shit was taking so long? His lawyer oughtta have been here by now. Must be sending some hotshot from Jeff City on account of the case he could bring against Chowder.

That must be it. Still hungry. Still thirsty.

MONDALE

He was still officially on personal time, but it didn't raise any eyebrows when he showed up at the station. He hadn't thought to bring a picture of baby Lilly and was kicking himself for that, but he got plenty of "grandpa" comments and slaps on the back from the day crew. He smiled at them until he'd shut his office door.

A moment later, there was a knock followed by Bob Musil entering his office. Musil shut the door and sat down. He leaned forward, elbows on kneecaps, and waited for Mondale to speak.

When they'd finished their pow-wow the deputy left.

The afternoon disappeared in a haze of small tasks he'd put off for too long. Vacation time, what a joke. Still, he felt better getting things done. It was going to be a long day and whatever he could eat up time with, helped.

CHOWDER

Hettie let out an involuntary gasp when her husband emptied the bag of cash on the bed. "What's it for?"

Chowder said, "Emergencies."

"What's going on, hon?"

"Pack up." He indicated the pile of cash. "It should be plenty to last us."

"Last till when?"

"I'm not sure, Het. Shouldn't be too long."

TERRY

They finally cut him loose around eight in the evening. His lawyer never showed, which was fine with him long as he got out. One of the deputies drove him home. They left through the station's back door and that probably should have sent up some red flags, but he was just glad to be going home.

Wendell wasn't there when he came through the door. There was hardly a sign he'd been there all week. Kid was damn near invisible. He'd have to call Beth's house in the morning and hope the kid picked up. If not, he could steal a car and pick him up at school, maybe. Regardless, his plan was to take his son on a real old-fashioned crime spree and for once he felt a swell of pride. Wendell had done well driving that first time he'd used him. Terry'd come out of the convenience store walking fast, the grocery bag lifting off the back of his head and another small bag in his left hand, two-hundred thirty-six dollars inside. A small score, but Wendell's first and he hadn't chickened out. Of course he hadn't, he was a Hickerson and had Terry's genetic code running through him. He could be taught. Terry just needed to give him some time and attention. Now that Cal was gone, that's exactly what he was going to do.

He found a half-full bottle of scrip meds for pain and swallowed four with a glass of tap water. Kid had finished off his beer. Good for him. That was more like it. He turned on the TV and flipped to channel fifty-one. There was Brother Eli wearing extra make up and sounding something less than his old self to Terry, but nonetheless doing a new program. He was talking about repentance and judgment, Sodom and Gomorrah, Jerusalem and Nineveh, send money and all manner of Bible places Terry didn't quite follow. He watched until the meds kicked in and he passed out sprawled across the couch in Layla's favorite spot.

MONDALE

He stepped out of his house at seven-thirty and locked the door. He was going to pick up Julie and take her to the Red Lobster in Springfield for dinner. He'd dressed in slacks and a jacket, then had decided that it made him look old and he changed into pressed blue jeans and a button up shirt with the sleeves rolled back. He'd wanted to leave his piece at home, but felt naked without it and ended up settling on an ankle holster. He hoped Julie wouldn't play footsie and blow his toes off.

When he turned to step off the front porch he saw Tate Dill watching him, leaning against a car parked across the street. He stood and waited for the skinny jackoff to walk over.

"Evening, Sheriff."

"Tate. The hell you doing at my house?"

"Need to talk to you."

"'Bout what?"

"The future."

CHOWDER

He came in through a jarred window in the back of the house. It was dark inside and smelled like a thousand kinds of decaying organic matter. The bedroom was empty, and he moved to the front room where the TV was on. He looked down at Terry Hickerson sleeping like innocence. Innocence trying to stuff busted fingers down the front of its pants.

TERRY

Something foul-tasting was being stuffed into his mouth. He tried to get his hand there to remove it, but it was useless, tied behind his back. What the fuck? He opened his eyes and saw Chowder Thompson standing over him with evil writ on his face.

MONDALE

Julie would just have to forgive him.

CHOWDER

He pulled over, popped the trunk and hauled the wriggling peckerwood out by his belt. The eyes were wide and he was straining against the socks taped inside his mouth. As much as Chowder wanted to just get this over with, he figured there was no harm in hearing the asshole's last words.

PART III

Dennis Jordan rounded the last corner to the homestretch of his morning run. His mind was clear and his conscience clean. Nothing like some physical exertion to wipe his psychic slate.

After his three-mile jog, he stripped down and hopped in the shower.

It was nearly seven A.M. and he needed to be in Springfield by nine to take testimony from a protected witness. Toweling off, his thoughts turned to Spruce and a reflexive smile spread across his face. He was immensely enjoying fucking with the policeman and the gangster. He'd be happy to prosecute either one of them, though without cooperation from one or the other it was going to be more work.

Charles Thompson's daughter Irma was a constant source of good material too. He'd been trailing her since Tate Dill had run into trouble in Olathe on a possession with intent bust and claimed he had important information to trade. Jordan's office had been called and with his nose for a solid resource, he'd made the drive himself and negotiated Tate's release. Dill hadn't been very forthcoming, but Jordan had sensed a potential goldmine and cut the little shit loose to scurry back to his hidey-hole and carry on fucking up. Meanwhile, Jordan kept his informant top secret. The only name Tate had really talked about was Irma Thompson, which had meant dick to Jordan, but Tate had claimed she was the daughter of a former Buccaneer and forever badass named Chowder Thompson who'd been running a quiet little business in the Ozarks for over a decade now. Tate had insisted that Irm was worth looking into, as she was eager to take up where her daddy had hung up the outlaw life.

Whatever. Jordan had looked into it, 'cause he liked to play the angles. If it didn't cost anything, why the hell not? He'd dug up records for Spruce, for Charles Thompson's businesses and property, tax records for the town and the leading citizens. He'd looked at arrest records and found Tate Dill's name attached to only one in his adult life, for possession of an illegal substance, which Dennis found hard to imagine. He'd met the little prick and seen his type often enough to know a habitual offender and opportunist when he encountered one.

So, he'd dug deeper. And he'd done it alone. As a politician, he was always looking for footholds and secret ones were always better.

And Irma Thompson had not disappointed. Her style was fast and sloppy-loose. She made her father look like a model of restraint and maturity. He'd staked out the Bait 'N More personally, and when she'd left in the middle of her shift that night, he'd tailed her all the way to her own stake-out of the Hickerson character. On the way there, a heavy rain had commenced and she'd sat outside his place, maybe waiting for a break in the storm, for a long time before the excited sounds of a dog and the slamming front doors of the pick-up parked in the drive had got her attention. He'd followed Irm following the truck out of town and stayed with her when she passed it up. Before long, she had turned around and he'd been forced to keep going, so as not to draw attention to himself. When she'd disappeared in his rearview, he slammed on the brakes and nearly went off the road, but recovered and turned around, killing his lights.

He thought he'd lost her until brake lights popped up, out of nowhere, a hundred yards in front of him. She was driving dark too. A moment later, the pickup came around the bend and Irm hit her brights, scaring the piss out of the oncoming driver, who swerved on the wet road and went right over the side a second later.

Turned out to be the sheriff's girl in the truck, and that was the wedge he was driving between his quarry: one's child had killed the other's. If Chowder didn't come to him in the next twenty-four hours ready to cut a deal, he'd take that information to Mondale and then sit back and watch the fireworks. He wouldn't need proof - there was enough tension in their relationship already. All he'd have to do is whisper to the high-strung sheriff and step back.

He hung up his towel the way his wife liked him to and came into the bedroom where his clothes were waiting for him, pressed and ready to go. From the back of the room, a gruff female voice startled him and he turned to see Irma Thompson lurking in the bedroom doorway. She said, "Morning, counselor."

He recovered without looking too foolish, no grabbing desperately to cover himself up. He worked hard enough at it, he knew he looked good. His nakedness was nothing to be embarrassed about. "Ms. Thompson? Did we have an appointment?" He flashed his Paul Newman smile, but it went unappreciated.

"Yup, but don't worry, you're not late. Just relax now." She started toward him and instinctively he took a step backward.

"I'm going to ask you to call my office next time you need-" He bumped into something that hadn't been there the moment before. He spun around and saw a very large man with long stringy hair and a Metallica t-shirt standing behind him. The man wrapped massive arms around his head and neck in some kind of sleeper hold.

Dennis Jordan struggled vainly against the man's grip, but the embrace was immutable fact and soon he felt himself slipping out of consciousness. As his legs failed and he went limp, the large man gently sat down with him on the bed. Irm hovered over him and spoke one word that swirled around and above as he felt the void reaching up for him, and he grasped at it like a drowning man, though it didn't seem to mean anything.

"Cinnamon."

CHAPTER TWENTY-ONE

MONDALE

Jimmy called Bob Musil and said he'd be by to pick him up. In the car he explained it the way Tate Dill had laid it out for him. Tate was taking over for Chowder with an outfit out of Kansas City. Chowder was done for, whether he wised up and fled the hills or stuck around and went to prison, he wouldn't be running shit by this time next week. Tate had found the K.C. outfit and approached them on his own, laying out the plan and letting them sniff around for themselves. And guess what? It looked A-okay to them. Worth investing in.

"So what's our play?" asked Musil, pulling up outside the back of the station where deputy Townsend was waiting, holding a shotgun in each hand and wearing his Kevlar and sunglasses at sunrise, badass via accessories.

Jimmy winced at the image, but it was better than the alternative: scared and unprepared. Without a word, Townsend opened the door and slipped into the back seat. He laid both shotguns across his lap and removed a Mountain Dew pop from one of the cargo pockets down the leg of his pants. When he cracked the tab and took the first noisy sip, Jimmy turned to look at him and received a thumbs-up.

Mondale addressed Musil across the front seat from him. "There's a meet 'n greet set up in an hour. I'll think of something by then." He started to put the car into gear, then turned back to Townsend again. A beat passed and the deputy, mouth full of soda pop, cocked his head slightly in a silent question, which Jimmy answered.

"Seatbelt."

TERRY

He had to ride in the trunk again. No socks in his mouth this time, though. Little better. He had all the way to Jeanette's house to think about his family and all the friends and strangers he'd caused to suffer in his lifetime. He didn't though.

CHOWDER

The pictures had made him laugh for sure. He hadn't known Eli's name, but as soon as Terry'd described him, Chowder'd known exactly who he meant. He was glad he hadn't killed the little shit without giving him a chance to talk.

Even if the money wasn't where he said it'd be, these pictures were worth something. Chowder reevaluated Terry Hickerson. He had balls - Chowder had seen the proof - and he had a plan. But he was just too stupid not to fuck it up. Hell, why was he sticking up Mexican liquor stores with his buddy while they were waiting on a big score to pan out? Because they were losers. Adrenaline cowboys. Get a little liquor or coke or crystal in em and they couldn't sit still.

The sun was beginning to peek over the horizon when they turned onto the street Terry had indicated. Chowder pulled up in front of the yard with the pickup. He looked up and down the street for signs of life before popping the trunk.

He hauled Terry Hickerson's skinny ass out and pointed him toward the front door. Terry nodded and led the way up the drive with Chowder's gun leveled at the base of his spine. Terry tried the door first, but it was secure. He reached into his pocket for something to pick the lock with, but Chowder just motioned him out of the way before expertly and easily busting through the old frame.

The noise wasn't much outside, but from within they heard that someone was now stirring from sleep. An elderly woman's voice called out, "Who's there?" Terry looked at Chowder and then answered.

"Terry Hickerson, ma'am. I'm Calvin's friend." They moved through the darkened front room, the musty smell of age assaulting their senses and growing stronger as they approached the back of the house.

"Calvin's not here," Jeanette called out. "Go away."

Terry and Chowder reached the bedroom and Terry paused before pushing the door open. Before them stood Jeanette Dotson dressed in a nightgown worn to near transparency and clutching a handgun that would surely break her wrists if she fired it. She gestured with the gun. "Go away," she repeated. Terry stepped backward and Chowder let him. When the old bat took a step toward them, Chowder reached for her hand and easily tipped the pistol out of her grip. "Oh," she said, and Chowder followed Terry into the room.

"Where's your diaper bag?" said Terry delicately.

Jeanette looked from face to face as if to decide whom she should be addressing. "What?"

Chowder bent to retrieve her gun and spoke in his gently commanding voice, "Calvin left something for us in the bag. He told us to come get it."

"Calvin's dead."

Terry went into to the bathroom, turned on the light, opened the medicine cabinet and began tossing the contents onto the floor. Then he looked through the cabinets beneath the sink and above the toilet. When he finished searching the room, he came back out and headed for the closet. He threw open the door and got on his hands and knees to rummage beneath the hanging clothes. "Where's the fuckin diaper bag?"

Jeanette just looked confused. Chowder gestured for her to have a seat on the bed and helped her ease down. Between the bed and a nightstand, Chowder spotted a vinyl toiletries bag. He reached down and picked it up. Inside he found a two-thirds full box of Depends, some wet wipes, ointment, baby powder. He took the box of adult napkins out and pulled the diapers aside. Behind them, he found a padded manila envelope.

CHAPTER TWENTY-TWO

MONDALE

The house sat off the gravel road up a dirt driveway fifty yards. It was impractical for getaway, but also impossible to approach unheard except on foot. Mondale made his way slowly up the drive, parked his cruiser and got out. He knew Bob Musil and Deputy Townsend had flanked the house by now and were positioned at the back door and side windows, but it still sounded stupid to go in. There were no lights visible, but he knew he'd find at least three armed men inside. The variables were hardly worth considering at this point.

He called out as he knocked on the screen door. "Sheriff's office. Open up." The silence that followed seemed to stretch on forever in the crisping autumn night.

"Fuck the police," came the eventual reply, followed by a nervous chuckle.

Mondale shifted his weight and straightened himself, hands resting on his belt and the handle of his service revolver. "C'mon, Tate. I got things to do." He heard three deadbolts sliding and a chain being removed before Tate's scruffy, gaunt face displeased his eyes.

Tate moved back, out of the sheriff's way. The inside of the clapboard shack was stuffy with a dampness that was all too ordinary even for the hour. A small rotating fan pushed the tepid air around like sweeping up a puddle. The wood floors were dark and scuffed with a collection of divots in one corner, the ghosts of dining arrangements from decades past. One ratty couch shoved against the wall and a single kitchen chair were the only furniture to be found.

There were three representatives from Kansas City, each wearing well-tailored suits and the usual collection of prison tattoos, crosses, eagles, swastikas and double lightning bolts, on their necks and the backs of their hands, tear-drops in the outer corners of a couple of their eyes.

Mondale spotted the bulge of shouldered weapons under their jackets and reflexively tensed his right arm. He forced himself to stand up straight, resisting the urge to crouch defensively and hooked both thumbs into the buckle of his belt.

Tate faded to the background, introducing only one of them: "Sheriff Jimmy Mondale, meet Zack Ryan."

The tall man with the long hair stepped forward, and said in a voice that sounded like gravel, "Tate says you're the man to see."

"Depends."

"We're willing to keep your current salary plus a half-percent. Throw in busts when you need them. Two or three annually, more in an election year."

"In exchange for what?"

"The usual arrangement."

Inwardly, Mondale bristled at that– peckerwoods assuming he and all law were for sale. Outwardly he smiled. "What about Chowder Thompson? He's a community fixture. Got sway with the bike gangs that want to move in. Got the whole thing consolidated and regulated." Then to the obvious point. "He's not going to just step aside."

Ryan exaggerated a slow exhalation of breath, as if explaining things to a child. "Tate takes over local representation with your cooperation. Everybody gets in line or fuck 'em. This deal comes with brand recognition."

"Big brand, though. Kansas City feels a long way off to most people here."

Ryan smiled humorlessly. "I know what you mean."

"Thompson?"

"Your responsibility."

Mondale's smile spread slowly till his upper lip disappeared. He shook his head. "I'm not a greedy man. Current arrangement is just fine. Never had a problem with Thompson either." He gestured with his chin at Tate. "Why are you so eager to back this cocksucker, anyhow?"

Ryan glared at Tate, and Tate stared hard at the spot on the wall just over Mondale's right shoulder. "Sheriff, maybe Tate here didn't explain things too good or maybe you've just been the swinging dick in a small pond too long to believe it, but this meet is a courtesy and nothing more." He took an envelope out of his back pocket and tossed it toward the sheriff.

Mondale let the package fall at his feet. "That's our buy-in and the one and only olive branch you'll see. We're here with or without your cooperation."

Mondale let his gaze sink to the envelope on the floor. Gingerly he crouched and retrieved it. His knees and back creaked and popped with the motion. The heft of the envelope was substantial. When he stood back up he employed both hands in the examination of its contents. He counted hundreds for a few more seconds before placing it into his own back pocket. "Well, thanks for this." When his right hand came back around front it was holding his service-issue revolver.

Tate jumped and sputtered. "Hold on there, sheriff. Come on now."

"Shut up, Tate." Mondale looked at the three men from Kansas City. He patted the envelope in his back pocket. "I'll keep this as a gesture of good will and it'll get you out of Hamilton County without hassle from police, but Thompson is not my problem, he's yours."

Ryan grew three inches standing still. It was a prison yard trick Mondale had seen before. Negotiations were just about over. "Thompson doesn't figure into our plans. We go through Tate." He stared hard at Mondale, telling him the way it was. "If you've got a problem with that–"

Mondale shot Tate through the top of his nose. The light coming from the single bare bulb on the ceiling of the cabin turned pink and the body dropped straight back without the top of its head. The men's suits were ruined, misted with gore, but their faces looked comfortable enough.

The stick and stink of blood was immediate, but no one moved to wipe it from their faces and everyone waited for Mondale to speak. After a moment of silence, he did in a measured, even tone.

"I've got a big problem with that."

TERRY

He watched Chowder open the package. He could see the biker counting money while the old lady watched, unsure she was in the right house. "What's going on," she asked. "Calvin put that in my bag?"

"Shut up," Terry said. He got up off the floor and approached to get a better look, but Chowder leveled his gun at him and Terry stopped.

"Sit down," the biker growled.

Jeanette spoke. "He left something for me? He left me money?"

Ignoring her, Terry said, "So? We're good?"

Jeanette went on, "That's my money. Calvin gave me that money."

Chowder finished counting and looked up, but not at anybody. Thinking.

Terry said, "C'mon, we should get out of here, split it in the car."

"Calvin loved me," said Jeanette. "He wanted me to have

that money."

"We gotta get movin," Terry advised, "and if you think I'm riding in the trunk again–" He never got the chance to finish the thought.

Chowder shot him.

CHAPTER TWENTY-THREE

CHOWDER

The old lady shit herself. The sound was a short, wet blast and the smell hit him almost immediately. "Oh," she said.

The redneck dropped onto his back with blood bubbling out of his chest. He looked bewildered. Chowder dropped the old lady's smoking gun onto the bed beside her and stepped toward her. "Lay down," he commanded, and she did. He was careful not to step in blood or shit as he reached behind her for a pillow. She lay down beneath him obediently, like she was at the dentist. She looked expectantly into his eyes.

"Calvin's dead," she offered.

"I know," said Chowder as he gently lowered the pillow onto her face.

MONDALE

Tate's expression looked as perplexed and ill at ease in death as it had in life. So much for resting in peace.

Zack Ryan held up a steadying hand to the goons from

K.C. and they waited for Mondale to continue. When he was ready to, he did. "Kansas City is not welcome here and Chowder isn't going away. You want to talk to him, stick around, but I don't think he's gonna give your offer a fair shake. He doesn't like being circumnavigated and neither do I." Jimmy put his pistol away and backed toward the door. "Like I said, this envelope buys you a free ticket out of town." He forced himself to go slowly and keep steady. "But if you ever come back, I'll shoot you and then say hello." Once out of the room, he turned around. He didn't make it down the front steps before the first shot splintered the screen door. Awkwardly, he jumped off the porch.

Mondale twisted his knee when he landed and he rolled clumsily under the front porch, dropping the envelope he'd just collected. White bolts of pain shot through his leg and were answered by surging adrenaline flooding his body. The men from Kansas City ran out the front door bringing enough fire-power with them to make him evaporate. He still had his gun out and used it, firing straight above him, blasting nickel-sized holes in the rotted-out boards of the porch.

The return fire chewed up more kindling, but Mondale escaped puncture. The whole world shook and he heard confused and angry yelling above him. The porch shuddered and collapsed behind him and Zack Ryan dropped into the dust. Cordite and dirt stung Mondale's eyes. Blood and bile filled his mouth. Half blind, he aimed at the Kansas City man's face and spent the last of his ammunition in three hot bursts.

His knee screamed at him as he tried to keep moving. So he stopped and lay flat on his back beneath a still standing section of the porch, rubbing his eyes, tears trying to work the dirt and blood out of his vision. The whole world was enveloped in a strong vibration that he surrendered to. He stopped trying to hear anything and squeezed his eyes shut. He felt the rotation of the earth speed up and he held on tight, trying not to slip off the edge.

CHOWDER

Hettie was waiting for him when he got home. She reported, "Safe is cleaned out, and we're ready to roll."

He patted her rump on his way through the door and continued on to the bathroom. Once inside, he sat down on the toilet. He called to his wife on the other side of the door, "Gas in the truck?"

"Shoot. No. Otherwise ready, Chowder."

Chowder was relaxed. "We need to stop by Darlin's anyhow. You can fill it, while I tidy up." He breathed contentedly and deeply and felt his bowels comply. It was going to be a bright, bright, sunshiny day.

CHAPTER TWENTY-FOUR

MONDALE

Musil's voice cut through the ringing inside his head. It sounded far off and underwater. "Jimmy? You alright under there?"

Jimmy stared up at the daylight struggling through the perforated lumber. He thought back to camping trips he'd taken with Eileen and Elizabeth when they were just kids, lying on their backs beneath the stars. He'd had to explain the universe and its order every night just to make sure it hadn't changed. *Jesus loves little girls and forgives daddies. Big animals eat little ones.* Lazy drips of blood found the holes in the porch and took their time pooling around the rims before drooling onto him.

Mondale finally rolled out carefully from beneath the rickety porch and stood, favoring his right knee, brushing sawdust out of his eyes and plucking a sharp, three-inch wood chip out from the back of his neck. It set off a blood flow that would ruin his shirt. "Shit. Somebody got a hankie?" Deputy Townsend produced a neatly folded silky piece that Mondale caught with his already-sticky right hand. "Thanks," he said as he applied it to his neck.

Bob Musil clapped his shoulder and said something Mondale couldn't hear, then went inside presumably to check out the basement. When he came out a few moments later, Jimmy's ears had popped and he could hear his deputy. "Bingo. All the fixings, just no product."

"S'alright, there'll be plenty of trace amounts on the equipment," said Mondale, stepping back into the cabin. Townsend followed and found him in the kitchen washing the blood off of his hands.

"That little turd on the floor sure looks surprised," the deputy observed.

Jimmy turned and regarded the still body of Tate Dill. "Shouldn't be. He was working toward this end his whole life."

Townsend thought that was hilarious. "I remember him from school. Thought he was slick shit." Jimmy's hands appeared clean and he looked around in vain for a towel, finally deciding upon his soiled shirt. Townsend, hopped up on Mountain Dew and violence, was pacing the tiny kitchen.

"Go on outside. You're making me nervous."

"Sorry, sheriff. It's just, *Whew!* What a rush, you know?" Mondale nodded his head. "You think we oughtta arrange something like this for Chowder Thompson too? I mean he ain't likely to –"

Jimmy hit him under the chin with his forearm and pushed until the young deputy was on his toes against the wall straining not to choke. His eyes were wide and white.

Jimmy whispered. "Let that be the last time you suggest a move against Chowder Thompson so recklessly. That man is evil you ain't even dreamed up yet, and his eyes and ears reach all the way up into your mama's snatch to hear your thoughts before you're born. So, for your own good and mine..."

He dropped the frightened deputy as Musil came strolling into the kitchen. "We're all set, Jimmy."

Mondale straightened and clapped his deputies heartily

on the back and shoulders. "Good. Let's light it up." They walked toward the door, Jimmy pulling Townsend along, the young man rubbing his sore neck. He turned toward Musil. "Bob, you see the way young Townsend here kept his shit?" Musil nodded. "I think he's got a future in gun fighting." He placed his fist encouragingly against Townsend's jaw and pushed. "Watch out, Doc Holiday."

Townsend's face turned red with pleasure, the parts that weren't already that color with pain and fear. His eyes held confusion.

They'd found enough accelerants among the raw materials in the basement to make sure the whole wooden structure was consumed. They dragged the bodies down to the basement and dug out the bullets not lodged too deep into bone. The house was old and dubious enough to have collected all manner of leaden projectiles in its history, so they didn't bother with the few misses scattered along the porch walls and roof.

When the explosion lit the fire, it went up bright and fast and the whole house was consumed inside two hours.

TERRY

What the fuck?

He'd been shot. That was what the fuck. Fuck. He coughed and tasted blood. He turned over and tried to stand up. No dice. So he crawled. He crawled over diapers and clothing and anything else that was in his way toward the front door. His strength, built on hate, propelled him toward freedom and independence.

He entered the hallway and tried to stand again. Almost. Not quite. He kept crawling. He focused on the front door, through which daylight beckoned. He'd get out and steal Jeanette's car. He'd drive home and get his son. Wendell would jump at the opportunity to drive and they'd hit the road, maybe stop for the night at a place in Oklahoma he and Cal had been to before. He'd teach his son how to shoot, how to intimidate a convenience store clerk and they'd laugh about it. He'd get a new dog too. Let Wendell name her and when he was healed up they'd go to a brothel in Stillwater he remembered. He'd call Beth sometime later so she could stop having a shitfit. Don't worry, the boy's with me and he's doing fine. He's doing good actually. Takes after his old man.

The daylight in the door darkened and a figure cautiously stepped inside. Oh well. Maybe he was headed to jail anyway. He could do a stretch. A short one. He may have been insincere before when he'd offered up Chowder Thompson, but that was before the cocksucker had shot him. He'd help build a case against that asshole in a heartbeat.

Terry's eyes couldn't focus on the figure now approaching him, but he could hear the man speak. "Where's the old lady?" he heard. If Terry could've shrugged, he would've, but he stopped crawling and lay on his back. The man moved past him and into the rest of the house. From the bedroom, Terry heard the man's exclamation, "Shit. Aw, fuck." And then he went through the rest of the house.

Terry closed his eyes and thought maybe he'd just take a nap. No sense in struggling any now. He'd wake up in the hospital or in an ambulance, already hooked up to a morphine drip. He could handle that. The man's voice was loud and angry. "Colton!" Terry opened his eyes and made out another shape standing over him. A smaller shape. A child. The edges were fuzzy, but Terry made out the Karate Turtles on the dirty cotton t-shirt looming above him. "Colton, don't touch him!"

Colton looked up to his father. "Call the am-blance?"

Colton's father stepped over and looked at Terry and though Terry couldn't say for sure, he thought the indistinct shape of the man and his voice were familiar. "Get out of here, Colton. Go home."

Colton turned to go and asked again, as he left, "Am-blance?"

"Fuck no," his father said. He looked down and Terry could've sworn he smiled. Terry felt the man's foot push down on his chest like an anvil. Terry saw a red spray and felt the blood spurt out of the sucking hole in his chest in a fresh new geyser. As he slipped away he heard the man say, "Not yet. He's still alive."

CHOWDER

He drove through the hills with Hettie beside him, a bag full of money with his Glock on top between them. They pulled into the trailer park and all the way to the back of the lot. Chowder left the keys in the ignition and got out of the truck. "You fill the tank while I tie up some loose ends," he told his wife, and he went up to Darlin's office door. As Hettie pulled out of the lot he unlocked the door and went inside. It was empty and Chowder muttered to himself. If that was the way Irm was gonna run things that was her problem. He was out.

He moved quickly, dismantling the credit card machine and clearing out files, such as there were. He went through the refrigerator as an afterthought, grabbing something for the road. He took the phone out of his pocket and made a final call to the sheriff.

Mondale answered. "What is it?"

"You get yourself witnessed?"

"Sorta. We clear on your end?"

Chowder grinned. "I took a monster bowel movement this morning, Jimbo." There was nothing on the other end of the line. "Yeah, we're good."

"Just keep your head low, for a bit, we oughtta be good."

"Don't let the Attorney get into your panties, alright?"

"Sure. You done?"

"Over and out," Chowder said, thinking to himself, you have no idea.

He hung up and sat down on the steps to wait for Hettie to return. He looked at the phone in his hand and considered calling his daughter to say goodbye.

CHAPTER TWENTY-FIVE

MONDALE

He stepped out of the shower and checked his fingernails. No blood or dirt beneath or around the cuticles. He checked his reflection in the mirror. The man staring back looked like someone else. The crow's feet were longer and deeper than the last time he'd looked, his skin was loose, and the ends of his mouth pulled back, sending wrinkles shooting toward his ears when he tried to smile.

He'd killed again.

It'd been years since he'd had to kill anyone and he hoped that he'd never have to again, but he'd seen it needed doing, and done it. And now, now he just hoped it had bought what he needed it to. He wanted the peace to hold. He wanted Chowder to run pussy and dope in a regulated environment without competition and unnecessary violence, without women disappearing forever or only to be found later in various states of decomposition. He wanted to assure a reliable tax base for his community. He hated the thought of outside syndicates pedaling in his town, soaking up the scarce resources of his citizens and sending their money out of town, out of the country. Buy local. Yeah.

His phone rang.

Against every instinct he had, he picked up. It was Bob Musil on the line. "Better get down to the station, Jim."

"Jim." Right.

CHOWDER

Hettie picked him up and they left. On the way out of town, he felt really good for the first time in too long. Hettie put her back against her door and plopped her feet into his lap. He fished his cell phone out of his pocket and threw it into a creek as they passed over.

MONDALE

The station was a flurry of activity. Inside, Federal agents in tactical gear with DEA printed across their backs and expensive sunglasses were everywhere. Mondale's mind raced for areas where he might be exposed, but he couldn't think of any. Mentally he ran through scenarios to explain their presence in his station and he didn't like any of them. He steeled himself for the worst and crossed the front room.

Bob Musil was at the center of a group of feds gathered around a map spread over a desk. He was drawing routes toward destinations marked in red. He looked up as Mondale approached. "Agent Harris, this is Sheriff Mondale."

One of the agents, a bulldog of a man, five foot eight and a hundred seventy-five pounds of upper body mass and a gleaming shaved head, extended his hand. Jimmy took it and said, "What's going on?"

Agent Harris spoke, "Sheriff, we had an undercover drop off the edge of the planet. His last communication put him in your back yard."

Jimmy's stomach dropped away. "Who was the target?"

The DEA agent said, "One Charles Thompson."

"Chowder Thompson?" said Mondale. "What's he mixed up in?"

Harris snorted, "Little of everything, it looks like, Sheriff."

Musil interjected, he looked ashen, "That crank-lab fire today? Bodies inside? Looks like one of them was Agent Harris's man."

Mondale said. "Guess my vacation is over."

Harris continued. "We're moving on Thompson now. Like it if you could come with, Sheriff."

"Of course," said Jimmy. "Give me one second."

He went to the bathroom and threw up in the bowl as discretely as he could manage.

CHAPTER TWENTY-SIX

CHOWDER

Hettie's eyes lit up when they turned off the highway before they'd even crossed the state line. "What's this?"

Chowder winked at her. "Proper honeymoon. 'Bout time, yeah?" Hettie looked unconvinced. "I got another stash house out here. You like it, we can hide from the world here a while. I got no powerful need to move, just to be gone."

MONDALE

From the bathroom, Jimmy dialed Chowder from his own throwaway phone. No answer. Shit. Chowder must've dumped his already.

He splashed cold water on his face and left the bathroom. He stopped and donned a kevlar vest and grabbed a shotgun from a wide-eyed Deputy Townsend. The young policeman looked panicked and Mondale ushered him into his office and shut the door.

Townsend sat down and put his head in his hands. "Is it

true Jimmy? Did we kill a federal agent?"

"Shut that down, son." Jimmy hissed. "All you did was back up your partner. You were there. It was kill or be killed at that point."

"But they say it was federal police we killed."

"I don't know if that's true or not."

"I think I'm gonna be sick."

"You just wait till we're out the door. You're staying here, Deputy." Townsend nodded and looked grateful and confused. "Can I count on you not to lose your shit?" Again, Townsend nodded. Jimmy left him sitting there and closed the door behind him.

When Mondale appeared in the front room again, Agent Harris called out to his men, "Sheriff Mondale will lead us out. This is his town and he knows the target." He turned to Jimmy. "After you, Sheriff."

Musil drove. Mondale sat shotgun and Agent Harris slid in behind them with the rest of Harris's men following in an SUV. Agent Harris spoke from the back seat. "Last report our man said his connect was setting up a meet with Thompson. Said that they were going in hot – that Thompson's reputation with the Kansas City syndicate was heavy, they'd been muscled out, as had Memphis, Little Rock and Tulsa."

Mondale nodded, "We haven't had any outside problems that I know about."

Harris went on. "After my agent failed to check in, the fire was discovered at the meet and we put eyes on all of Thompson's businesses. We picked him up, cleaning house. Looks like he's making a run for it."

Mondale and Musil traded looks.

"Tailed him to an unmarked road." Harris reached over the seat and indicated the location on the map circled in red. Mondale squinted. He didn't have any idea what Chowder might be up to there. He hadn't driven that old mule path in years. Old cabin falling apart at the ass end of a winding, rut-pocked dirt road. "Pretty isolated, so we're meeting up with the tail car at the road's start. You have any ideas about his purpose in that area, Sheriff?"

"Not really. All I know of, if it's still standing, is a cabin about a mile in. Land was bought up for back taxes by an out of town acquirer maybe five years ago. Never heard of anybody doing anything with it." Mondale turned around to see Harris's face. "Sorry as hell to hear about your man, Agent Harris."

The agent's features were hard and the action of loading his shotgun, rolling the cartridges between his finger and thumb were as automatic and ritualistic as a prayer. The fed looked back at Mondale without breaking the rhythm of his work. He shrugged. "We lost a good man today, and I, for one, am looking forward to this. Cocksucker's getting what he's got coming."

CHAPTER TWENTY-SEVEN

CHOWDER

The cabin used to stand at the base of a hill, but Chowder might describe it as leaning, now. Hettie's look said *what the fuck?* Her mouth said, "You're the boss, boss man."

Chowder chuckled. "I'm just fuckin with you. We're not stayin here. We'll cross the state line, find a motel with a porno box and mirrors on the ceiling. I just gotta tie up one last loose end." He put the truck in park and got out. Hettie, behind him, slipped her shoes back on before stepping into the yard and stretching.

"Mmmm, just like old times." She followed Chowder around the side of the dilapidated structure, careful to not strike a foot against any of the old and treacherously located rusting junk settled into the mud and patches of high grass, checkering the yard. On the shack's far side she found her husband scanning the hill, then fixating on an irregularly shaped mound of earth. He began to walk toward it, picking up a discarded steel pole from the ground as he went. "What you huntin, Chowder?"

"Dale something."

MONDALE

The entrance to the road was blocked by a black SUV. That one plus their own cruiser and the vehicle following them made three conspicuous vehicles clogging the tiny entrance. Musil stopped the car and Agent Harris jumped out. Mondale followed the DEA man to the agent waiting for them at trail's head.

Musil came up behind him with a string of three more federal police bringing up the rear. Agent Harris spoke to all of them circling the hood of the first agent's SUV. "Sheriff says there's a cabin about a mile in. Says the condition of the road is poor. I believe that we'd make too much noise driving in. Couldn't go more than ten or fifteen miles per hour anyhow. So everybody grab your gear. Agent Phillips stays here to cover the road and I don't want any radio communication that isn't strictly necessary." Harris made eye contact with each man standing in the circle. "Make no mistake, gentleman: Agent Ryan spent a year undercover with Kansas City and today we will finish the work he died doing. We want a strong, clean case, but most of all we don't want to spend one more good man's life taking out the trash. Do not hesitate to use deadly force if you have to." Each agent gave a nod of understanding and Harris slapped the hood. "Let's go."

CHOWDER

It had taken only twenty minutes of scratching the dirt with the steel pole to uncover Dale something's remains. Fuckin Irm. Lousiest disposal job ever. Tate had found it easy enough. He'd probably dug him up then pushed the dirt back over just to demonstrate to Chowder what a joke it all was.

Dale was unrecognizable. Elements had been at him. The lime had helped, but it was still obviously human remains and inexcusably sloppy. He told Hettie to go wait in the truck and she hadn't taken any convincing. He tugged on the arms to pull the body out of the dirt. He yanked and the body moved just a couple of inches, yanked again and nearly lost his footing, a strip of flesh tearing away in his hands.

It took another twenty minutes, but he brought Dale's remains into the shack in three trips, piling his bones on top of three bags of charcoal Hettie'd picked up from the Bait 'N More. He used a hammer to bust the teeth out of his mouth and picked what shards he could and threw them into the back yard. Hettie'd also brought a shelf full of lighter fluid, which he liberally soaked the pile with. He then went room to room spraying the accelerant over every surface. The fumes were making him lightheaded when he exited onto the sagging front porch.

Out in the air the smell was faint and he took a few moments to take deep breaths to clear his head, then he went to the truck for a box of matches. Hettie was dozing in the last lazy moments of sunlight and he put his hand on her shoulder, rousing her gently. "Hey," he said, "Gonna miss the show." He took the unopened box of matches and strode to the front porch and removed the cellophane casing. He removed a single stick. Struck it on the side of the box. The flare was bright and then died down. Chowder tilted it downward to coax the flame up, then dropped it into the box. Three seconds later a second bright flare followed by a quick succession of them and Chowder gently lobbed the flaming box into the front doorway and stepped back.

A tide of blue fire spread over the porch and he saw it traveling down the hallway. Chowder ran backward toward the truck, watching the pyro-show, and reaching the still-open driver's door just as a brilliant flash burst through the windows, shattering what glass remained in the frames. Then, like the individual match, the flare died down and the burn commenced in earnest.

He turned to his wife, smiling like a kid watching a Fourth of July celebration. But Hettie wasn't smiling back. She was lifting the Glock.

CHAPTER TWENTY-EIGHT

MONDALE

They moved at a quick pace, walking silently over the un-even road, avoiding holes and obtrusive root formations. The light was dying, lost in the thick tree-line. In another hour the trip would necessitate flashlights.

Bob Musil strode beside him, trying to disguise his heavy breathing, but the overweight deputy was sweating profuse-ly and had to constantly mop his forehead with a kerchief. Mondale made eye contact with his best friend and saw de-termination hardening over the fear beneath. He guessed that Musil saw the same mixture in his own face and turned his gaze forward to avoid it being detected by any of the resolute federal agents with them.

When he recognized the road's last bend before the cabin was visible, he held up his hand for the procession to stop. Agent Harris stepped to him and Jimmy whispered the in-formation. Agent Harris rounded the bend with Mondale signaling the others to wait for them to return.

Around the corner the cabin was visible fifty yards across

a clearing. Chowder's pickup was parked in the muddy drive, twenty yards away from the front porch. Harris told Mondale to stay there and went back to the waiting men. While Jimmy crouched behind a rock he saw Chowder come out the front door. Jimmy looked over his shoulder. Agent Harris wasn't back yet. Was there any way he could warn Chowder without tipping off the feds?

Chowder was opening the driver's side door, but not climbing into the truck. Mondale sent a psychic message to the old outlaw.

Turn around. See this coming. Run away now. Disappear.

Nothing doing. Chowder retrieved whatever he was fishing for and began walking back to the cabin.

Agent Harris appeared at his side again, this time with three more federal agents and Deputy Musil in tow. Harris whispered to all, "We can't let him get into the truck. No time to fan out. Follow me." The agent stood, as did his men, who spread out as far as they could on the narrow road and into the clearing. Bob Musil locked eyes with Mondale, and nodded. They followed suit.

Chowder threw a small flaming object into the open front door of the cabin and stepped back. The agents slowed their approach. Agent Harris stopped altogether. Chowder began to back up toward the truck and Harris saw that his chance at nabbing his man without incident was beginning to evaporate. He motioned his men forward and was at a trot when the heat from the blast singed their eyebrows. At twenty yards, shotgun leveled, Agent Harris called out, "Charles Thompson! On your knees, asshole!"

They were Agent Harris's last words. The back window of the truck's cab exploded with bullets and Harris caught one with his mouth.

CHOWDER

Hettie's eyes were cold and her intent to kill was plain. Chowder heard his own name called and then Hettie opened fire. The world was an inferno of glass and bullets, fire and blood. He turned to see Armageddon in flack jackets descending upon him, led by Jimmy Mondale atop a pale horse.

Hettie was empty and reloading when the windshield turned red. She fell out the passenger side, one hand clamped over her neck and a fine spray of blood shooting between her fingers. The next shot caught her high in her right shoulder and spun her around and the back of her head burst like a water balloon in the next instant.

Chowder screamed for her, ignoring the angry voices ordering him to show his hands. Something big and unseen hit him in his side and his right arm stopped responding. He looked at his attackers, chose one and ran straight at him.

CHAPTER TWENTY-NINE

MONDALE

Agent Harris was dead before he hit the ground. His face had nothing behind it anymore. What used to be there was all over the man to Jimmy's left. The pulp-blinded agent dove to the ground to avoid more bullets while he scooped his boss out of his eyes.

The agent to Mondale's right opened up with his shotgun on the unseen shooter inside the truck. The agents fanned out, putting as much distance between them as possible, forming a semi-circle around the truck. In four seconds the firing from inside the truck stopped. Bob Musil dropped to one knee and fired into the shattered back window. There was a grunt that punched through the sounds of thunder around him, then Chowder Thompson screaming himself hoarse.

A woman, shit, Hettie stumbled out the passenger side door with one bloody hand clamped to her neck. She slammed the butt of the Glock on her thigh, securing a fresh clip, but, as she raised her arm to fire, she spun one hundred eighty degrees and the back of her head disappeared in a pink mist. She fell forward onto whatever was left of her face.

Chowder screamed with renewed fury and the agent on the ground next to Harris's corpse shot the outlaw in his right side, ripping meat from the bone of Chowder's arm and opening up small holes near his ribs. The biker staggered, leaning on his left foot, before charging at the man to Mondale's right.

Jimmy threw his gun to the ground and dove for Chowder, hitting his partner across his tenderized chest and shoulder and knocking him to the ground. He landed on top of Chowder and held on for all he was worth. The big man was trying to get to his feet even as bullets tore up the ground around them.

Staying on top of Chowder felt like riding an electric current. Jimmy squeezed with his arms and legs as his business partner bucked and rolled and kicked and thrashed beneath him. Jimmy caught bites of sound: the burning house in front of him snapped and crackled and threw off intensifying heat, the agents ran to the fallen bodies of Agent Harris and Hettie Thompson and were beginning to assist him in subduing Chowder Thompson.

Bob Musil used the butt of his shotgun on Chowder's chin to stop the struggle. The biker went slack and Jimmy rolled off of him.

The agent with Harris was on his radio calling for an ambulance and frantically relaying their coordinates. Jimmy lay on his back in the hard clay beside the unconscious figure of his partner, wondering how long he had left. How soon would they come to his house or the station and place him under arrest? Would he have another chance to see his granddaughter before it all came down on him? Would Irm retaliate in the night, waking him up with a knife through the eye? He looked at his deputy. Bob. What would happen to Bob? He would try to leave his staff out of it. Chowder had been right. The town, his family and his own police force would turn on him. His intentions would never matter to them. He'd done dirt. The worst kind. And they'd crucify him for it.

Musil reached a hand down for him and Jimmy gripped the meaty arm and hoisted himself up with it. He threw his arms around Musil and whispered to him, "You say what you have to, Bob. I'm not taking you down with me."

Musil gripped him tightly. "Hold it in. You don't know what'll come of this."

Jimmy let go of his deputy and found a rock to sit on. He eased himself down and looked into the sky. The first stars were just visible on the far edges of the horizon, but the fire was washing out the night sky above him.

Musil took command of the scene, organizing the feds and emergency traffic that was beginning to bottleneck on the road. Jimmy watched paramedics revive Chowder Thompson and their eyes met across the smoke and confusion. Chowder wore an oxygen mask, preventing him from speaking. Jimmy sent him psychic messages:

It wasn't me. We're still partners. We can work something out. Please don't bring it all down.

Murder was all he got back.

EPILOGUE

CHOWDER

Chowder Thompson sat in the conference cell, waiting for his visitors. He'd not uttered a word to any of them, except the name of his lawyer. A case as high-profile as his, the feds would be on their best behavior, none of the usual dirty tricks. No leaving loopholes for his lawyers or the media to exploit. He didn't have to wait long. Over the course of several weeks, he'd had regular meetings with his council and a defense plan had begun to form.

He looked up now at the sound of someone at the door. The guard who entered didn't look Chowder in the face and as soon as he had admitted Chowder's lawyer and Irma Thompson, he exited. Chowder looked at his visitors.

"Well?"

His lawyer produced a pack of cigarettes and a lighter and placed them on the table in front of his client. "Their case is almost entirely circumstantial. Plus their guy, Harris, was running a pretty loose ship. The whole operation was a long way from textbook. Depending on what they choose to prosecute, they'll most likely be fighting countersuits against the agency, plus the major focus was Kansas City. You were sort of a side project."

"So what does that mean?"

The lawyer continued. "I don't think they want this to go on any longer than we do. I think a plea bargain is a real possibility."

"How much time are we talking about?"

The lawyer shrugged. "More than you're going to want. Two federal agents died." The lawyer looked at Chowder, trying to read his client's features. "But maybe not as much time as you think. The DEA is going to be held at least partially responsible for those deaths."

"You get my package?"

The attorney nodded. "Yes, though, I'm not sure what you want to do with them." Chowder smiled to himself, thinking of the photographs of a famous televangelist sucking cock he'd had the foresight to send to his lawyer.

"I think we could find Shekina Ministries very interested in my defense is all. Friends with deep pockets are always worth having."

The lawyer made a note. "How would you like me to approach them?"

Chowder lit a cigarette and inhaled deeply. "I'm not sure yet." He exhaled a plume of blue smoke and said, "Lemme talk to Irm in private."

"Sure. Is there anything else you want me to do?"

"Just do your law thing. Keep me appraised." The lawyer stood and nodded his goodbye. He knocked on the door and it was opened a few seconds later by the guard. Chowder and Irm watched the attorney leave, then Irm spoke.

"I think I've got somebody else eager to help."

"If you'd just done what I asked you to in the first place. Whole fuckin world knew Dale Kube was rotting behind the cabin. If I hadn't stopped, your momma…" He gave up reprimanding his girl. A lump formed in his throat and his eyes misted, but he said nothing.

Irm's face was red and she spoke in a terse whisper. "You want my help or not?"

Chowder stared at the table. After a moment he took another drag on his cigarette. Irm continued. "Just listen to me."

Chowder raised his gaze to meet his daughter's. His genius daughter who was gonna save the day. He couldn't wait.

Satisfied that she had his attention, Irm began at the beginning. "Now you remember that big girl workin at Darlin's?"

Chowder shook his head and shrugged. "No."

Irm continued. "Well, her name's Cinnamon."

MONDALE

He got up every morning expecting to find his house surrounded by federal agents. He went to work keeping an eye out for black SUVs in the lot, but weeks had passed without his world ending. Deputy Townsend took personal time and told Jimmy he was going to start looking for a position out of town. Mondale told him he'd write a letter of recommendation.

Every day after work, he spoke with his best friend. The Musils had him over for dinner and he and Bob stayed up drinking like it was the last supper. They arranged contingency plans, but day after day, nothing came.

Every morning he called Liz and talked about the baby and he cavalierly made plans to come visit at Christmastime, plans he never expected to happen, but that felt good in the making anyhow.

The second night, after Chowder Thompson's arrest, he showed up on Julie Sykes' front porch. Her bedroom light was on, but she never answered the door. He left an apology note in her mailbox. On Sunday afternoon, he called her at home. She didn't pick up, so he spoke to her machine like she was listening, the way Shirley used to do with him. He'd gotten all the apologizing he intended to do out of his system, and let her know he wouldn't bother her any more. If she wanted to see him, he'd like that. She knew where to find him.

He'd gone to see Beth Moore, Terry Hickerson's ex-wife. He'd sat down with her and told her how Terry had died, shot by Cal Dotson's aunt Jeanette when he broke into her home. Jeanette Dotson had apparently died of the excitement. If he ever spoke to Chowder Thompson again, he was going to let him have it for the old lady.

Wendell Hickerson had come home in the middle of the death notice. His mother asked him to come sit next to her on the couch and listen to what the sheriff had to say. Jimmy'd looked in the kid's defiant stare and not been able to hold eye contact. "I'm real sorry to have to tell you this, son."

He'd been interviewed by the DEA endlessly, and gave the helpful, if clueless, local rube routine till he thought he'd choke on the words if he had to repeat them one more time.

The morning Assistant State's Attorney Dennis Jordan showed up in his office, Mondale took a deep breath and exhaled through the palms of his hands and soles of his feet. If this was it, he was ready, but he thought he'd like a chance to knock out one of those perfect teeth first. Mondale let him in and shut the door behind him. The lawyer took a seat in front of Jimmy's desk and the sheriff sat down behind it.

The ASA was dressed sharp as always, but didn't carry himself with the same arrogant prick-sure style as before. He didn't look Jimmy in the eyes as he spoke. "Sheriff Mondale, I'd like to ask you some questions about Agent Harris and the events of the day he died."

Jimmy cocked his head. "I've been through all this with the DEA."

"I'm aware of that, Sheriff, and I've read a copy of your testimony, but I have some questions of my own. I am filing suit against the Federal Drug Enforcement Administration on behalf of Charles Thompson and the late Hettie Thompson."

Jimmy said, "Come again?"

CHOWDER

He sat in his cell and wrote journals. He documented every-thing he could remember about Jimmy Mondale and The Bucs. Any detail or event that crossed his mind went into the books. At each weekly meeting, his lawyer would collect them and supply him with more empty volumes to fill.

The plea deal was beginning to take shape. Looked like something he might get through. Once out, Jimmy Mon-dale could suck his dick. He'd fucking own that town and Mondale's badge. When Irma came by, he'd coach her if she wanted it, which she did sometimes. She had a long way to go, but she was learning.

Once she brought him some pictures to see. Ones she'd told him about. Seeing them made him smile. They were of the big girl, Cinnamon, he remembered when he saw the photos. They depicted her sexing with a movie star looking fucker that resembled very closely the Assistant State's Attor-ney, Dennis Jordan. Kinky shit.

He'd shuffled through a half dozen pictures, all taken from the same angle, to appear like a hidden camera, but clear and revealing plenty of detail. He handed them back to Irma. "You done good, girl."

"Thanks, Daddy."

"And hey, that Cinnamon?"

"Yeah?"

"Give her a raise, huh?"

This book would not exist without all the encouragement and ass slapping I received from my earliest supporters, editors and publishers: Cameron Ashley, Greg Bardsley, Laura & Pinckney Benedict, Frank Bill, Paul D. Brazill, David Cranmer, Peter Dragovich, Kent Gowran, Glenn Gray, Jordan Harper, Brian Lindenmuth, Matthew Louis, Keith Rawson, Todd Robinson, Kieran Shea, Anthony Neil Smith, Steve Weddle. Thank you.

Scott Phillips, thank you.

Thanks also to the Noir at the Bar community, especially Rod & Judy – you guys rock.

Finally, for the family members and close friends for whom association with me has cost dignity, respectability and peace of mind: I hope someday it pays off. No promises.

ABOUT THE AUTHOR:

Jedidiah Ayres is the author of Fierce Bitches and A F*ckload of Shorts.

CPSIA information can be obtained at www.ICGtesting.com
Printed in the USA
BVOW02s0959061115

425952BV00003B/136/P